MW01253340

LAVA

LAVA
and other stories

GILBERT REID

TWIN RIVERS
PRODUCTIONS

This is a work of fiction. Names, characters, places, and incidents either are products of the author's imagination or are used fictitiously. Any resemblance to actual persons, living or dead, events, or locales, is entirely coincidental.

Copyright © 2019 by Gilbert Reid

All rights reserved. No part of this book may be reproduced in any form or by any electronic or mechanical means, including information storage and retrieval systems, without permission in writing from the publisher, except by reviewers, who may quote brief passages in a review.

Issused in print and electronic formats
ISBN 978-0-9953108-0-3 *Lava and other stories*: Paperback
ISBN 978-0-9953108-1-0 *Lava and other stories*: EPUB
ISBN 978-0-9953108-2-7 *Lava and other stories*: Kindle

Cover and text design by Counterpunch Inc. / Linda Gustafson
Cover image courtesy of NASA

Published by
Twin Rivers Productions
20 Bloor Street East
PO Box 75070
Toronto, Ontario, M4W 3T3

gjreid@gilbertreid.com

Visit http://www.gilbertreid.com/

for Elena Solari

To me every hour of the light and dark is a miracle.
    ...
Each of us inevitable;
Each of us limitless – each of us with his or her right
    upon the earth.
        ...
I am of old and young, of the foolish as much as the wise ...
    – Walt Whitman

I declare
That later on,
Even in an age unlike our own,
Someone will remember who we are.
    – Sappho

Contents

LA DOLCE VITA

Lava

For
beauty is nothing
but the beginning of terror …
– Rainer Maria Rilke

"IS THAT LAVA?" It was a woman's voice, throaty, just above a whisper.

"What?"

"That." She cleared her throat and stretched one lazy arm, pointing. Even now her skin smelled of sun and perfumed soap.

"What?" The journalist turned heavily in his chair, following her gaze.

At night the hills burn; the air is heavy with smoke; but, in the darkness, except for a watery stinging in your eyes, you can't see it. The burning hills are steep. They rise like mountains, up from the sea.

Below the hilltop town, down by the shore, from the terrace of a luxury hotel, from a restaurant patio, from a beach, or from a swimming pool, you can look up. High above, in the hills and mountains, you will see thin dull lines of fire.

The smoke is perfumed like grass burning, bitter-sweet and strangely exhilarating. It takes you away from where you are to somewhere else, to somewhere elemental and inhuman, somewhere more dangerous than where you are, or seemingly so.

"Lava," she leaned forward. "Is it lava?" She had ash-blond hair and was about forty-five. Since at least age sixteen she had been described as "one of the most beautiful women in the world."

And she was indeed a great beauty – even now. She would – or so the magazine articles implied – be a great beauty until the day she died.

The journalist was overweight and sweating heavily. Hot sticky liquid collected in the thick folds of his belly. Twisting heavily in his chair, he followed her pointed arm, and blinked at the darkness. "Why, yes. Why, yes. I believe it is: yes, lava."

High in the air, at least fifty kilometers away, hung a twisting worm of light. It glowed red, a red-hot wire – insistent, pulsating, as if alive.

"You can see the lava, but not the stars," the actress said. "It must be far away." She shuddered. It gave her, she realized, a subtle voluptuous thrill: the great volcano rising towards the sky, towering, invisible, in the night – sending forth a river of red-hot lava.

"Overcast," he looked up, "It's the haze perhaps – the smoke from the hills."

"I think I'll try to get some sleep." She shoved back her chair.

"It's too hot to sleep."

"I have air-conditioning. I'll put it on."

"Air-conditioning is bad for you."

"Not sleeping is bad for you too." She smiled, stood up, shook his hand very lightly, and was gone.

The journalist watched her go – she had a casual, sensual stride. She didn't look back. The journalist glanced around. Suddenly, without the glitter of her celebrity, without the focused intensity of her cool blue eyes, the café terrace, covering a third of the piazza, seemed bigger than before, emptier – desolate.

A waiter, in a white jacket, stood in a corner, at the edge of the terrace, next to the entrance to the café, arms folded, yawning. Under the lamps of the piazza the round white metal tables looked like dull pools of stale milk.

A banner hung over the entry to the Corso, the narrow, pedestrian, main street: *"Festival Internazionale del Cinema 1979 ... "*

The journalist got up and walked to the parapet. He leaned his elbows on the metal rail, still warm from the sun, and stared towards the invisible volcano.

Along the parapet, on a line of short stubby metal pillars, stood a row of slender brass telescopes, tilted down, and blind.

Far below was the sea.

The journalist turned his back to the parapet and leaned with his elbows against the railing. His shirt was soaked; he was sticky all over. On the table lay his open notebook. A hot flush of hatred flooded up his chest and infused his face. The cool indifference of the woman had obliterated him, reduced him to nothing. She had been perfectly polite, seemingly relaxed, but icy cool; he might as well have been an insect. Some people merely have to yawn and they turn you into shit.

Is that lava? The bitch! In her coolness, she had been cruel without even realizing it – wealth did that. Wiping his forehead, he narrowed his eyes, wealth, and beauty too, and fame, and power in all its unconscious and insidiously evil forms.

The last image – her walking away from him – echoed in his mind: the low-heeled sandals; the casual, undulating stride; the perfect naked legs; the tight white cotton skirt, the famous figure and the carefully coiffed blond hair, one strand casually loose at the nape of her neck – even a goddess must show a touch of human imperfection; it made the performance even more persuasive. He wondered what it would be like to be her – to be a woman like her – with tits, ass, and legs like that, with a face like Helen of Troy's, destined to launch a thousand ships – to be a beautiful woman who was rich, who had had many illustrious lovers, and who had been famous for years – no, fuck, for decades, she'd been famous for decades!

He wiped his forehead. Imagining what it was like to be somebody else was a weakness, a form of vertigo, a bad nocturnal habit, vicious and addictive, a self-indulgent ritual of almost masturbatory intensity; he had never grown out of it – putting himself in the skin of somebody else, anybody else, man, woman, or child – but women, especially women, beautiful women.

Vertigo, whirlpool, maelstrom.

He scratched his crotch. He could so easily disappear into his own imaginings. One day he might lose himself forever. It used to be his strength, these leaps of corporeal physical empathy, plunging into the inscape of another's mind, into a stranger's body and sensibility; now it was his weakness. He could envisage things, *see* things; he could, in truth, *be* things ...

Shit!

He shifted his weight and for an instant imagined his elbows pinioned, tied, roped to the parapet railing. A sensual flood, an ecstatic abandonment, rushed over him; his body was transformed, it became another body; a momentary transfiguration. *Je suis un autre.*

Saint Sebastian, pinioned and pierced by the arrows, the loincloth barely concealing ...

Simple narcissistic masochism, it was no more than that.

He'd read all the books; he'd diagnosed himself; he knew what he was: *I am my own pathology; I am my sickness; that's what I am.* Yes, his life was a sickness, incurable, endemic.

Soaked with sweat, his shirt clung close, wrinkled and itchy and pasted heavily to his back. It was stifling. He wiggled his shoulders. He couldn't breathe, he had drunk too much. Yes, he drank too much; he was overweight; he was sweaty, unshaven, and filthy; he was indeed a miserable specimen. Oh, yes! Oh, yes! And, yet, once, oh, yes, once he had been such a pretty fellow – such a pretty fellow indeed. And now? And now what was required was a soliloquy, an ode to self-abasement. He cleared his throat. Yes, look at you now ...

Yes, look at you, now, Nuncle: dry infertile flaps of flesh for tits; wizened nipples, triangles of sagging flesh; a belly that is a belly merely, drooping outrageously, an unfruitful, flabby, flatulent coil of gut. What are you, man or woman, spirit or flesh? *Oh, Omphalos, untie me from the center of the world, the unwinding umbilical cord ...*

Shit! What shit was this? This pretentious bullshit, this hyper-consciousness, this self-indulgent, downward spiraling self-absorption, this melancholy hall of mirrors! What a labyrinth! Shit. Shit. All shit!

All the old ambitions rose up, the old ghosts: What about that great novel he promised himself he would write – the prose poem that would include everything, yes, everything: It would include, encompass, and embrace the whole fucking universe and all its fucking tastes and smells and sights and sounds, all its sublimities and banalities, all its infinitesimal details and vast unfathomable cosmic truths; it would, with relish and ease, conquer the biggest themes and the smallest itsy-bitsy frivolities, forever and ever, amen – and now he knew he never would write the damned thing!

Fuck, fuck it!

It was the desire to be God! That was it, the ambition to rival the Creator. Hubris. Ah, you are in truth an obscene capering monkey, grasping beyond your reach. Fly too high, too close to the sun, Icarus, and your wings melt, and you come crashing down.

With relish, he rubbed his sweaty hands. This was going to be a maudlin night. *Tra la, tra la, la, la ...* Self-pity. It was a tune he delighted in: An utter failure was what he was, and that's what tonight was too! SNAFU, utter SNAFU. Failure at dusk, failure in the twilight. And who cares! *"Fuck it!"* This time he said it out loud.

The sleepy waiter in the white jacket looked up.

"*Fuck him, too,*" the journalist snarled. He turned away. His first book of poems was the only good thing he'd ever done in his whole goddamned fucking useless life. In any case, the book was not very good at all: a few clever *aperçus*, one or two good lines, a couple of words tossed off when he was drunk sitting in a Parisian café and feeling sorry for himself because some girl had stood him up – his muse! She was a cheap slut with beautiful, half-closed almond eyes, a pale thin face, and scarlet lipstick, who'd flirted briefly with him in a cinema queue, place de l'Odéon, and, so, without knowing it, she had become his muse – his cruel perverse sadistic unknowing muse. She had possessed his soul absolutely, and she had no idea she had done so! And then he got himself published. Hey, presto! Abracadabra! I'm a genius! See what a vast sensitive soul I have! *Soul!* That's a laugh! The girls were eager to sleep with you then, eh! You could fart, and belch, and have halitosis and dirt between your toes – it didn't matter, they'd love you and fuck you just the same. Then, after a few years, a few bottles too many, a decade of bottles too many, and puff, poof, piddly-poo, all gone!

All gone! There ain't nothing no more ...

Dort und da. And then – Nichts.

Nothing ...

Nothing can come from nothing ... Nuncle ...

He turned back towards the invisible sea. *Now I am nothing!* And with that formula of self-annihilation came a sudden surge of exhilaration – sensual arousal – phallic stirring – *nothing, abject, cast down, naked.*

He hiccuped and wondered. Were the great mystics such sick hopeless souls, and the flagellants, carrying their weight of sin and self-inflicted scars, the wooden cross, the whips, the dripping blood?

Everything was pathology in the end – even salvation, even life, a sickness merely ...

He moved away from the railing and back to the café table and glanced down at his notebook – at his scribbled quotes from the actress. She'd been so cool. She'd used such casual, controlled phrases, so calculated. Whatever else she was, the bitch, she gave a good interview, clearly pre-shaped in her mind, just enough intelligence deployed to intimidate, cultivated but not too cultivated, totally in control, and so cool. Her English, too, was superb, and her Italian, and, of course, her French.

In France, she was an icon.

Beautiful ...

And then she had to show off – how beautiful, happy, successful and rich she was, how happy with her life, with her ... She did it with subtlety too, carelessly and with truly classy indirection, little nudges, mere nuance, but still ...

Hatred – a surge of hatred. Torture – his mind could imagine many forms of torture: she was more than merely intelligent, much more; she would be a magnificent victim; she would fight back, tooth and nail; and she would appreciate, oh so acutely, oh so delicately, all the subtle gradations of her hideous mutilation, of her slow annihilation.

He hiccupped.

Sweat dribbled down his back; his head ached and his legs throbbed. He looked around. His hand, as he raised it to his unshaven chin, began to tremble. He felt like shit; he looked like shit, he was shit, he needed a drink; he wanted to die. *The bitch!* It was envy, simple envy ... and maybe something more.

He hiccuped.

Beauty – a reminder, a *memento mori*.

He picked up his notebook and moved away from the table.

Envy, gluttony, sloth: one sin entails another. Envy begets gluttony begets drunkenness begets lust. Was lust a sin? He couldn't remember. Do not covet something or other – thy neighbor's ass?

He felt like a cool gin-and-tonic or like emptying a bottle of hot whiskey, pouring it over his head, gulping the hot amber shower.

He stood in the hot rain – In the hot rain he stood, Tiresias of the flabby tits ...

A golden shower, now that would be something, a proud tousle-headed, deeply tanned all over teenager doing the splits over you – blond bush dripping wide open, and ...

Prophetic and blind, in the hot rain, a seer you are ...

Naked, the wind rising, calling prophecies to the ...

Gusts, the hot ...

Flatulent gusts ...

Eructations in the wind ...

Piss on it, you filthy-minded slime-covered groveling masochistic white-bread fat-assed sadist whey-faced motherfucker!

Ah, even your self-hatred is histrionic, a farce, a performance, admit it, you clown, nothing you have ever done or said has rung true, nothing, not ever.

Nothing comes from nothing, Nuncle.

Oh, yes, my Fool, how true.

He gnawed at his knuckles and glanced back towards the railing, towards the darkness over the sea, and towards the volcano – invisible except for the meandering line of lava, the worm of light pulsating, glowing-ember red. Yes, he thought ... how did it go?

The invisible worm
That flies in the night
...
And his dark secret love
Does thy life destroy.

And then ... something, something ... He turned away from the distant lava: the pulsing worm. The image, for a moment, danced, then drifted, in his eye, the drifting worm. *Yes,* he thought, *yes, the insidious all-consuming tapeworm of love ...*

∞

It was late and it was hot but the great man, who was very old, was still up. He was wearing a white panama hat and with his walking stick he pointed at each of the shuttered and darkened shops as they walked up the steeply sloping cobblestoned street to the ruined Greek theater on the promontory.

"That one was very good!" he said.

"That one was sweet," he sighed.

"That one was very accommodating. Very accommodating indeed." He stopped and frowned.

"What's he talking about?" in a whisper the young man asked the great man's assistant.

"Boys," said the assistant.

"Boys?"

"Years ago the guys who own these shops were boys."

"Oh."

"Decades ago. Maybe a hundred years."

"Oh."

"They were very good boys too," said the great man, who habitually overheard every word.

"Times change," said the assistant.

"Times change indeed," said the great man. "Oh, now that was a wonderful moment!" He stopped in front of a small shop, which apparently sold ceramics; he lifted his cane and pointed at the bolted-down metal shutters. "That, if you will allow me to say so myself, was pure ecstasy, an epiphany."

Somewhere a siren sounded.

∞

Not far away, the underwater pool-lights looked like blurry blue moons floating in a rippling and very relative universe. Bubbles rose and sparkled all around him as the man glided smoothly, his arms thrusting, plowing the water, striving, his lungs bursting, striving to the limit, as his chest skimmed an inch above the chalk-white bottom of the pool – striving, striving, striving – his heart hammering, striving, striving, striving. He would make it to the end of the pool without once breaking surface, four full lengths. A defiant bet, as always, with himself.

Finally, in a spray of blue water, he burst into the air, gasped for breath, hooked his fingers over the slippery edge, and gulped air, desperately gulped air, gulped air. With each breath he smelled the smoke from the hills, raw and sweet – a smell from far away and long ago.

He let go of the edge of the pool and for several long minutes he floated easily on his back and breathed the blessed, dangerously redolent, perfumed air.

He pulled himself up, swiveled around and sat on the edge of the pool – already feeling the heat as the rivulets of cool water ran away, sticking in sparking drops to the hair of his chest. His legs dangled in the cool water.

The pool and terrace lights floated, echoing on the cobalt surface, in loops, circles, ovals. Soon, like the stagnant air, the water would settle down, and lie still. He took a deep breath – again, the smoke from the hills. It came from long ago and far away; it came from other places, other times, and other lives.

The day she died the air had been smoky too.

A beautiful perfumed haze had drifted out over the sparkling sea.

For a brief moment he remembered – he *saw* – how she stood on the terrace-balcony, her dark, shoulder-length hair, a bright smile, tight blue jeans ... At the last minute she raised her hand, saluted, and grinned and waved – *goodbye, goodbye, goodbye ...*

Dead now – how long? Three years, two months, and ... some number of days. He'd lost count.

When you lose count that's when things are ending.

Even now, he could picture it: her jeep, she had swung it wide – as he learned later – at a sharp corner to avoid a herd of goats. The shoulder of the road was too soft, weakened by recent torrential rain. The soil gave way. The jeep toppled, went over the edge of the cliff, and went down, tumbling, down, over and over, down, and down, and down ... And exploded, and burned.

Caught between two outcroppings, the crumpled jeep had burned and burned, a fiery furnace. When they reached it, of what remained there was nothing that could even vaguely be called human.

Sometimes he felt that he had died with her, many times, and come back to life, each time moving a little farther away from her. After each rebirth, there was a new life, a new man, a little less of the man he had been before, a subtle betrayal of her, and of himself.

And yet he was the man he had been still.

He was the man he had been, yes; and now, briefly renewed, he was ready for whatever life might offer.

∞

The Journalist closed his eyes. *Yes, yes, yes ... it was the right poem – Blake, William Blake.*

And his dark secret love
Does thy life destroy.

The journalist walked to the metal railing and looked out into the darkness. Forty or fifty kilometers away, the worm, the bright coiled string was a glowing ember, a piece of festive scarlet Christmas tinsel, hung in the night sky. In reality, it was fifteen kilometers of lava – a kilometer wide – curling down the mountainside.

The shirt stuck to his shoulder blades and his belly. His crotch was gluey, itchy, his penis limp, curled in on its own impotence. He wondered if he should have another gin-and-tonic now – or later. *Or the whiskey? Ah – the whiskey!* Maybe he should just go to his hotel, down on the shore, lock himself in his room, strip, take a shower, and scratch the itch.

He looked back at the table; too charming, she was, the simpering blond bitch, too fucking charming. Of course, she had been famous since she was 12 years old, and she knew how to handle people ... *Manipulate,* that's what people said; that was the verb: *manipulate. The bitch!*

Directly below the parapet, terraced gardens plunged down, then steep vineyards, then, far below, invisible, the rocks and the sea.

The journalist strained his eyes, but he could see nothing of the sea, nothing at all. He took a deep breath. The air was immobile, hot and heavy, clammy and close, with the smoke from the hills.

∞

"This one was particularly exquisite," said the great man in what he suddenly realized – standing outside himself for an agonizing instant – was an excessively precious, high-pitched voice – even for him. The revelation was displeasing. The voice unveiled too much of himself – or, rather, it revealed the wrong part of himself – or, rather, one of the wrong parts of himself. There were so many! Was it the queen, the bitch, the southern belle, the frustrated housewife, the incurably precious hysteric, the satin-clad hooker – which one? He wiped his forehead and glanced around. It really didn't matter. Whoever it was, it revealed too much of himself to himself – and to others too. To that young man for instance. The great man frowned. In his long life, he had adopted so many voices, so many selves, that it was difficult to tell which voice, which self, was his own. Or perhaps he had no voice that was his own? Maybe all the voices he spoke – or who spoke through him – were equal, each voice, each self, being a world unto itself – the bearded sage, the spoilt tearful whiny brat, the caring fussy hysterical mother, the obsessive hypochondriac of indeterminate sex and interminable complaint ... Each voice in turn occupied the stage and for a moment displaced all the others, and all the bodies too, all the imagined bodies into which he poured himself. Of course, it was his talent – the ventriloquist-like talent of a great playwright; or, perhaps, in reality, he was a shaman, possessed by spirits, forever on the threshold of yet another mystic epiphany of abnegation and abandonment. He poked at the pavement with his cane. So what persona now? What mask?

The cultivated and dissolute esthete? Yes, perhaps that was the best role for this particular occasion.

He stood now, the great man, stout and shrunk about the chest, a wide belt holding up his oversized trousers, his panama tilted back, and he waved his cane at another storefront. "Now that! That, I must say, was wonderful – black curls tight on the forehead, clear dark skin, a nose chiseled by the gods, and a body – hairless and all smooth delicate nut-brown muscle ... Like a little girl, like a muscular little girl."

All the stores were closed and the metal shutters were bolted down tight. Large ceramic vases, decorated in yellow and white and blue and green, stood outside each shop.

"Souvenirs," said the great man, tapping one of the vases with his cane. "Memories ... Of course everything is changed now. They are not the same." Suddenly he smiled.

"He takes a malign pleasure in the fact that those boys are no longer boys," said the assistant, tilting his head at the young man.

"Yes," said the great man, dreamily. "In those days they were like gods. They swam naked, lay on the rocks in the sun, wore laurel leaves or vine leaves in their hair, and nothing else. They smiled as quickly as a girl would smile. Eager to please. Such beautiful teeth! Such brown smooth skin! Such beautiful smiles! They seemed entirely unselfconscious. I was jealous of them even then, I suppose."

"And now they are middle-aged bald ex-gigolos with spaghetti bellies, fat wives, five grown children, and several grandchildren," said the assistant.

"Was my love merely jealousy? Was it false even then?" said the great man. "Mere jealousy? Even then?" He turned to the assistant. "In any case, you are wrong. They are not middle-aged. They are old men now."

∞

Il Festival Internazionale del Cinema 1979 ... It would all start tomorrow; there would be time enough ...

She closed the brochure and slid off the bed. On the commode stood a vase with six long-stemmed red roses and next to the roses a cornucopia of fruit wrapped in tight transparent plastic. She smelled the roses, ran her fingers over the cool plastic, went to the French doors and looked out.

The glass doors gave back her reflection. She turned the ornate gilt handles and pushed the doors open. Her reflection – and the room – swung back in a quick cubist flicker and disappeared, her own ghost fleeing, leaving her alone with the night.

She took a deep breath. Her heart skipped a beat. She closed her eyes. What was it? What was that feeling? Ah, yes, it was the smoke.

It was the smoke that touched her; the smoke from the hills – an acrid, burning smell, sweet like burning sage.

Like an Indian cigarette, like the smell of the blazing sunlight and heat of India, and that tour boat outside Bombay and the little boys leaping high in the air, their shoulders and backsides gleaming for a moment in the sunlight as they jumped into the harbor; and she was leaning on the railing in the glittering sunlight and clinging heat, the hot sea-breeze blowing the cigarette smoke, swirling it away from her lips; and she inhaled the exotic smoke, closed her eyes, and felt dizzy with longing ... She'd gone out to an island to see some damp, mud-colored sacred caves, with voluptuous big-breasted goddesses carved out of the rock, and a sacred lingam standing erect and proud, a phallic god, inside the arched entrance, and she felt then that, somehow, the older polytheistic religions were better, richer, deeper than the new simplistic monotheisms – it was merely an impression; and she knew that – theologically speaking – the impression was unfair and one-sided, but the sensual richness of the place, the openly displayed sexuality, the abundance, the polychromatic splendor, the dazzling sun-lit inclusiveness, appealed to something deep inside her: "Everything is sacred, nothing is divine." Whatever the hell that might mean. That's what she felt. That night she'd dined with the famous Indian actor, a tall handsome thin fellow, her costar, and afterwards they drank too much wine and made love in his suite and ...

Tonight it would be difficult to sleep.

She stepped from the doorway onto the balcony. The garden below was a dimly lit formal pattern, with neatly cut hedges and geometric pathways; it stretched down towards the pool, a brightly lit island glowing in the dark – pure cobalt blue, brilliantly shining.

A man was sitting alone on the edge of the pool, his legs dangling in the water. Behind him the land plunged, invisible, to the sea. Above the sea there was darkness, no stars, no moon. Not yet.

Interviews left her emptied. They were a performance like any other. But, as the years went by, they seemed more and more a tawdry sham. Her life, when she explained it, was a lie. The things she didn't talk about were the crucial things. It occurred to her – and not for the first time – that her own desires, her own self, would remain a secret until the day she died, a secret even to herself. The unexamined life ...

She crossed her arms. If she never shared her most intimate thoughts and feelings with anyone, she would never have lived. Not really lived.

Bring on the violins! She frowned.

She ran her hands down her sides, over her breasts, feeling that tonight it was another woman she was caressing, not herself.

Tonight, even her body was a stranger; even her body was not her own.

I'm possessed. Tonight I'm possessed.

She was reputed to be an ice goddess, as cool as cool could be; but, left to herself, in her most intimate moments, she knew that, whenever the opportunity presented itself, she gave away to moments of shameless excess – shamanistic self-abandon. Her hunger for intensity was so great.

If life is a lie, what, then, can love be?

What does it mean – to *live* a life?

Life was a performance, a ritual, a dance, a pantomime, it was shadow boxing; it was theater; phantoms argued with phantoms; masks sparred with masks; and, if it was all a charade, what became of truth? And without truth, how could there be love?

Love would be a lie.

Lying became a way of life. It *was* a way of life; it was *the* way of life. She was an actress. That's what she did, she lied: she performed.

Every word, every gesture, was an act, a performance, a lie, a script. It was habit-forming. Words were inadequate; they could not unmask such lies.

To be is to perform.

To perform is to be.

Life is theater, after all, all the world's a stage, and all the men and women merely players ...

Or was life just one big long interview? An interview with oneself – the tales you told – the tabloid version of yourself – and just as false as the interview she had just given to that unhappy man – the journalist? What was his name?

The image surged up: She could see him – oh, too, too clearly: His face blistered with booze, his small wet pink lips twitching, and his blue eyes foggy, clouded, skittish and evasive. She could imagine that, once, not so long ago, those eyes had been a candid and innocent blue, the skin smooth, the features chiseled and handsome, not blurred into perdition. His hair was thick, greasy and unwashed; circles of sweat had spread under the armpits of his wrinkled shirt, with its fine vertical white-and-blue stripes. He'd been so unhappy. There was something obscene about his unhappiness. Unhappiness of that degree was indecent, self-indulgent, a weakness; it should be hidden, veiled, like the genitals. In reaction, and unable to resist, she'd begun to parade her own success; she'd pirouetted, flaring out her elegance, and she had hated herself for it: *I am a bloody sadist, a miserable cruel show-off!*

Perhaps that's what she had always been.

Feeling an inner chill, she hugged herself and turned away from the invisible sea. High in the darkness glowed the burning coil of lava, pulsating, alive. Holding herself closer, she watched the worm of light, fading, brightening, and fading ...

A worm ...

A worm that gnaws

And empties the heart ...

She stroked her bare arms. Maybe people who believed in God felt they were really known, really loved for what they were, what they *really* were, and that, in the eyes of God, all mystery, all dissembling, fell away, and, in the eyes of the Lord, who knew and saw everything, the believers truly existed, existed truly.

They could kneel, pray, be known, be forgiven – they could *be*.

Perhaps people believe so they can feel. So they can exist.

She returned to the room, turned off the air-conditioning and stood in the French doors. The hot smoky air moved into the room and against her skin.

∞

The lovers had taken a room high in the hills in a modern cheap hotel on an outcropping above the hilltop town. They were pretending to be discreet. Adultery in that part of the country in those days was dangerous.

The hotel was almost empty. They went up the modern marble staircase and made love in a high-ceilinged, bare room – white ceramic tiles, white marble floor, white window frames, and a big flat hard bed. It was the sort of bed that is a platform to make love on, not a bed to sleep in. The balcony looked out at nothing but the night sky. In the distance, the coil of lava was like a worm glowing in the sultry dark. The man wondered what would have happened if he'd been afraid of heights? The woman was afraid of nothing.

∞

The journalist had a few more drinks and left the café. He wandered down the main street of the town. The Festival would start tomorrow night. Only a few people had arrived. The main street

– the *Corso* – was narrow and twisting and dark and most of the bars were closed.

Under the lamplight the black cobblestones glinted. Overhead, between the close overhang of the ancient two-story buildings, a few banners stretched limply. *Festival Internazionale del Cinema ...*

Light spilled out from the deconsecrated little church halfway down the *Corso*. The journalist stopped on the threshold. Workers were installing the festival press center – fax machines, typewriters, and rows of telephones. The day after tomorrow it would all start humming. Posters were everywhere.

Festival Internazionale del ...

The journalist went to the bar opposite the church and sat down. A golden sliver of light fell on the cobblestones; the bar was one of the few bars still open, a narrow hole in the wall, really. He sat at a small table out on the street and ordered a double Johnny Walker Black Label without water and with just a touch of ice.

Sounds of hammering came from the church. Over the entry to the church was a small statue of the Madonna, blackened by the years, and smoothed by the sun. It looked as if it had been carved out of ebony.

The journalist stared at the statue and at the banner hanging across the narrow winding street. "*Mastroianni, Deneuve, Duras.*" He ordered another double whiskey and sat still, letting the sweat dribble down his back.

∞

The woman wanted to make love on the floor, so they lay down on the cool white speckled marble. The smell of smoke filled the room and on her skin it mingled with her perfume and sweat. He licked the salt of her breasts.

"Do you love me?" she asked.

"I love you."

"How much do you love me?"

"As much as there are stars in the sky or drops of water in the ocean," he whispered into her ear. The standard answer seemed to give her the standard pleasure. He didn't know why she always insisted on asking the same questions.

"What do you mean by love?" she said.

High in the sky the worm of lava glowed.

∞

The great man sat on one of the stone bleachers high up in the ruined Greek amphitheater and tossed a small pebble. It bounced on the rows of stone bleachers lower down. "Once everything was sacred," he said, "Every single thing."

"Oh, oh," said the assistant.

The young man looked at the assistant and then sat down on a stone bleacher higher up and at a certain distance from the great man.

Down below on the stage a small circle of light marked the spot where some workmen were preparing the theater for the show the following night.

Festival Internazionale del Cinema 1979.

The Greek Theater was a great semi-circle of stone and the ancient Roman wall, which served as a backdrop behind the stage, was shattered, gaping open in the middle. Beyond, almost in the center of the stage, the coil of lava, fifty kilometers away, hung, gently vibrant, dark as a dying ember.

A worm, glowing red in the night.

"In Bali at dawn the young women carry offerings down to the sea. Floral designs. And they leave small floral offerings on the thresholds of the houses too." The great man was staring into the night. Above the theater, on a block of rock overlooking the sea, stood the guardian's house; it was a square building with no visible windows, a cube of gray stone. Like a detail from a painting by Corot, creamy white and insubstantial, thought the young man. Silhouetted next to it was a single dark cypress.

"Bali. I know about Bali," said the assistant.

"Pantheism," said the great man.

"I know, I know," said the assistant.

"This pebble is as real as anything there is." The great man turned a small pebble around in his fingers.

"Of course," said the assistant, rolling his eyes.

∞

The actress turned off the lights and undressed in the dark. She left the French doors open. The warm smoky air drifted in as the cool odorless hotel air leaked out.

She splashed her face with cold water from the sink, turned on a small bedside lamp, and lay down on top of the covers to read.

A small pile of books and newspapers occupied the left side of the king-sized bed. "Let me see, which of my lovers shall I have tonight?" She closed her eyes and picked a book at random. "Henry James! *Merde!* How dreadful. Why did I bring that?"

She dropped Henry James and picked up a book called *Advanced Poker Strategies*. Lazily, she turned a few pages.

∞

The lovers lay side-by-side on the flat hard bed. He ran his hands over her body as if he were reading some secret in the curves and slopes. She was a beautiful woman and he wondered why she needed so many words to assure her of his love. He was madly in love with her but frightened of her passion and her unpredictability. She had needs and ranges of emotion far beyond what he knew or felt – and far beyond what he knew he could ever know or feel.

She had insisted they make love on the balcony, which they had done, hanging over the empty space.

As they made love he was facing down over a sheer one hundred-foot drop and he could hear voices from another room and see couples strolling on the narrow panoramic path twenty feet below. She made a growling noise in her throat which quickly rose to a scream, and he had to jam his forearm in her mouth to stop the people on the path from looking up or the other people from coming out on their balconies and looking down. She bucked up underneath him, and scratched his back, deep stinging marks of red. "I adore drawing blood," she whispered. Hours later he would still have teeth marks in his forearm.

The doors to the balcony were still open and he could hear the voices from below and smell the smoke from the hills.

He was envious of the normality of those voices: the voices of people strolling in the calm of the evening, voices not trapped by passion. They were normal people going to have a beer or a glass of wine on a terrace. They were men not enslaved by the most beautiful woman in the world, men who would wipe their foreheads and talk of the heat and watch the women walk past; and the women would talk of the heat and of dresses and shoes and children.

She turned in the bed and smiled at him. The irises of her eyes were green and speckled with mica and shards of gold, as beautiful and impenetrable as the eyes of a tiger. "Do you love me?" she said. "How much do you love me? What do you mean by love?"

Far away the lava burned.

The invisible worm
That flies in the night ...

∞

"The ancient gods were best," said the great man. He turned the pebble between his fingers. "There were so many, so many ancient gods."

The young man looked up at the cypress, just visible, silhouetted against the sky, and at the blind walls of the guardian's house, gray stucco vaguely luminous – perhaps it was Gustave Courbet he'd been thinking of, not Corot, the painterly almost dream-like quality of the walls, perhaps Cezanne, early on, or Derain, André Derain: stucco walls offering a form of visual presence that was almost tactile. He looked down at the workmen, in a small circle of light, working on the stage. Above the workers, hanging in the sky, was the string-like trace of lava, a worm of glowing lava. It looked like it had been arranged, and put there on purpose, part of the decor.

"Testing, testing, *prova, prova, prova*," said a voice over the loudspeakers. "*Uno, due, tre, quattro, prova, prova.*"

"Gods on a human scale, with human passions," said the great man. Stiffly, he stood up. His belly bulged, pushing his belt outwards. "What you find in love, each time you find love, if you really find love, is a god. And each time it is a different god."

"He gets this way sometimes," said the assistant, "late at night." He raised his elbow, miming drinking.

The young man stood up, brushed off his trousers, straightened the creases, and noticed a veil of white dust on the points of his shoes; he walked down a few steps. He looked at the assistant and then at the great man.

The great man had turned and was smiling at his assistant, but it was difficult to tell if it was a smile of hate or love.

∞

The actress put down the book, stood up, and stretched. She pulled on a pair of shorts, slipped on a blouse and a pair of sandals and left her room.

The long corridors and broad stairs of the immense ex-monastery were empty. At the desk, the night porter and his assistant bowed and smiled. *"Buona sera, signora. Fa caldo."*

"Buona sera," she smiled. *"Si. Fa caldo."* She walked through the empty bar and restaurant and out into the garden and towards the pool.

The man was still sitting on the edge of the pool, his legs dangling in the water.

"Is the water cold?" She crouched to scoop some of it up.

"Cool," he said, "Cool enough."

She slipped out of her sandals, sat down at the edge of the pool, and slid her bare legs into the water. She shivered.

"You'll get your shorts wet."

"It doesn't matter."

He turned his head to look at her. Very nice legs, he thought. He examined the profile and realized that the face was a famous face, a face you saw on posters or in glossy magazines, a face that advertised expensive perfumes. It was a face that seemed already familiar, seen for many years, as if she were an old friend.

"How long is that lava flow?" She nodded towards the glowing ember.

He looked up. "About fifteen kilometers. As of this afternoon."

"Is it dangerous?"

"Here?"

"Anywhere." She nodded towards the mountain. "There."

"Not if you're careful. Not usually. The flow's coming out of a long crack in the side of the mountain. It's moving slowly. It's fairly viscous. There's a village in the way, but they've evacuated everybody. The lava moves slowly. It can be dangerous if you get too close. There are small explosions, hunks of rock, hot gases."

"Is this volcanic rock? Here, where we are now?"

"No." He looked around. "Where we are – this is an outcropping of a mountain range, an ancient tectonic folding."

"Tectonic ...?"

"Tectonic plates. There are a number of fault lines, just out to sea, running between here and the mainland. It's an earthquake zone. There are tremors here every day. Most of them too small to be noticed." He made a model with his hands, one palm slipping under the other, curling the fingers of the upper hand to represent the heaving up and folding of mountains. "The African tectonic plate or bits of it have been pushing north east, and are slipping under us, under the European tectonic plate. Right here the African plate is being pushed down. Long ago, during the clash between these continental plates, this range was pushed up and folded over. We're perched on the edge of the African tectonic plate, and close to where the tectonic plates have shifted back and forth; so the rocks here, long ago, were folded, buckled, and turned over, and rippled up under the stress."

"You know a lot about it."

"Enough."

"The cicadas don't stop. Even at night."

"No."

"It must be the heat." She splashed water on her face. It dripped down onto her blouse.

"Yes. The heat." He splashed some water on his arms. "I used to think it was a romantic sound, the cicadas. Years ago. You know, the south, the Mediterranean, the pagan gods, the hot volcanic earth, the old mythologies ... all that. Now I'm not so sure."

"No. Familiarity ... "

"... breeds contempt."

She half-smiled. "... not entirely. Not always ..." She splashed more water on her face, tilted her face upwards, let the water run down her neck.

"No. Not entirely. You're right. Not always." He scooped up water and splashed it on his chest and arms. "It's like the volcano. You study her for years, but you are never sure what she's going to do next, you never develop contempt. Or you shouldn't. Contempt is dangerous."

The actress looked up at the glowing string of lava and then at the man sitting next to her whose dark skin and hair were silver with drops of water.

"Would you like a drink?" he said.

"A drink? Yes. Yes, I think I would like a drink."

"I'll phone for one. What would you like?"

"I'm restless tonight. I don't know what I'd like." The actress smiled and moved her legs in the water. Water splashed up over her shorts.

"It's the smoke." He held her gaze. "The smoke is nervous. It makes us restless."

∞

The journalist stood on tiptoes in the middle of the street and spun around, stretching his arms out. *I am pissed out of my mind, pissed out of my mind, and, Oh Mother of God, but it feels good.* "Oh, the pain, the pain," he whispered, "Oh the nails, the nails hammered in, the nails, the dripping blood, the sacred stigmata! I am Christ, I am God!"

He stopped his pirouette and, bowing the heavy-bellied bow of a corrupt Renaissance courtier, he stared up at the Madonna. "Oh, Mother of God, I your son implore you ..."

"Ma, che fai, bello?"

One of the Festival officials was standing in the church door. "What on earth are you doing, my handsome friend?"

"*Niente*. Nothing." The journalist cleared his throat. "I was stretching."

"*Bene*. Good. I'm glad it's nothing." The man smiled. They had known each other, casually, off and on, for years. The man was one of those perfectly tailored, perfectly coiffed, tanned, handsome burnt-out Italians who have seen everything, forgiven everything, done nothing, and seem to have no emotions whatsoever. "Time to go to sleep, I think, my boy, no?"

"Yes, yes. You're right." The journalist picked up his glass – his third – and emptied it. His hand was no longer steady. The whiskey burned his throat, still burned, even now.

"*Fai attenzione*. Be careful."

"*Si, si, si.*"

"*Niente scherzi*. Don't do anything foolish."

"*Oh, io ... tu sai ...* Oh, you know me ... I never ...*"

"*Buona notte.*"

"*Buona notte.*"

As the journalist walked down the dark street the Italian stood watching him: The poor fellow was not very steady and he was very unhappy, lurching this way and that. *Yes, some Englishmen – or was he American? – They really can't handle ... Italy, perhaps Italy, perhaps the dolce vita, perhaps ... the cheap wine of course, and the women and the boys, perhaps the boys, the Mediterranean, the old gods, and the heat, of course, the heat ...*

The journalist didn't look back. He concentrated on cleaving to his course. *Steady as she goes, old man, steady as she goes!* Everything seemed too bright, too real, too intense – the store fronts, the cobblestones, the limp festival banners, the air itself; all of it pressed in on him, pressed in on his prickly skin, his aching eyeballs, his raw nerves. "Fuck it, fuck it! Fuck everything! Fuck them all, each and every one."

Above him, a drooping banner hung. "*Duras, Mastroianni, Deneuve.*"

Soon he was weaving back and forth, from one side of the narrow street to the other; he was drunk, and playing at being drunk, putting out his arms and pushing himself away from the walls, reeling out into the center of the *Corso,* and then back again.

Without warning, a high narrow stone arch loomed up in front of him, the gateway to the town. Beyond the open gate stretched a narrow paved road, a rough stony field or two, then the precipice – and the cable car which would take him down to his hotel on the shore.

"So much wisdom," he shouted, "so much wisdom!"

He threw his notebook in the air.

"Fuck, fuck, fuck!"

As it came fluttering down, he caught it, with a pirouette and an almost delicate sweep of his sweaty hand.

∞

"Senile," said the assistant. "That's his problem. He's senile." He nodded at the great man.

The young man stared.

"Senile," repeated the great man with an exaggerated moue of distaste. "The trouble with him is he's senile," he mimicked the assistant perfectly, in a mincing voice, and then turned to the young man. "Don't mind him. We do this all the time. He's my clown. Or I'm his. I'm not sure."

"Maybe we'll never know," said the assistant. He kicked at a pebble. "Who is who, I mean, or which is which."

"Love, when you get old, you see, is like vaudeville," said the great man. "It consists of routines known by heart. You know those old couples? You see them all the time. They quack at each other. Quack, quack, quack!"

"Quack," said the assistant.

With his cane the great man pointed at the dark shadow of the cypress. "Now that's something holy, a holy tree, a black flame. It's like the soul, a flame-like void, an absence, an illusion: the inky tip of a painter's brush – the mere touch of nothing; it is that nothing, the very concept and manifestation of nothing, of absence, that illuminates everything that exists, all that is and ever shall be. Ah, yes, indeed, the calligraphy of nothing. There's nothing there to see at all. It devours the light; it makes me think of cemeteries. I'm sure you've noticed those couples. In resort towns. In Florida. Everywhere. She wears bright colors, pink running suits, sandals or sneakers. Her bottom is too big. Her breasts have sagged beyond repair. She has no shame. She flaunts the ruin of her body. Such contempt! And the man! He wears flowered shirts, baggy trousers. He vaunts his impotence, his helplessness, his dentures, his toupee. They are ..." The great man bowed towards his assistant.

"... a standing joke for each other ..." said the assistant.

"... a routine always on stage, never ..." The great man bent to poke at some moss between the stone steps of the theater.

The assistant grinned. "... never not for one minute ..."

"... themselves ..." said the great man.

"... afraid to be ..." added the assistant.

"... themselves ..." The great man straightened up.

"... they wouldn't know what the self was if ..." The assistant yawned.

"... they bumped into it ..." The great man examined a piece of moss on the end of his stick. "So you see the way it is, young man."

"Nothing is original."

"Everything is lost."

"Even love."

"Above all."

"Love."

"If you only give it."

"Time."

"*Voilà!*" The assistant bowed.

"*Voilà!*" The great man curtsied.

∞

"Depends how viscous it is," he said.

The actress looked at him closely and wondered how much vodka was in the vodka tonic.

Sparkling drips of water like silver planets, transparent sparkly little moons, were caught in the black hair of the man's shoulders and chest.

"If the lava is viscous it solidifies quickly, forms a sort of giant cork, you see." He made a tent with his hands. "Pressure builds up. The more it's repressed, the more the pressure builds up. The inclination of the volcano's sides become steeper. The pressure forces the sides out. And then ... Boom! It explodes."

She glanced up towards the volcano, invisible in the night sky. Only the string of lava glowed ember-red, dimly.

He narrowed his eyes. "Pure energy. Lava will take almost any form the terrain will give it. And cool and crystallize and take on a crust. Or explode. Lava is fluid; then it solidifies." He glanced at her. "Rather like the human soul."

"Like the soul?" She raised an eyebrow.

"Oh, just a comparison, a figure of speech. When you think how different people are ... how they are formed by different pressures, different forces – like fluids that cool and freeze; they lose their fluidity and become solids – they become like stone."

"Yes. People *are* different." She twisted her lip, bit it, and looked away.

"The energy is like a fluid in the beginning – then it grows crusty, just like people. People crystallize, they become like – *things*. They forget that once they were fluid, that once they were free; that once, before they froze into their present shapes, they could have taken another form, lived another life. They might have become some-one else." He swallowed more of the vodka tonic and looked at the woman's legs in the pool. The legs, which she barely moved, danced with the dancing of the water, shifting loops of light. Her shorts were totally soaked now, transparent. She'd been famous for a long time. He again wondered how old she was: must be forty, maybe for-ty-five, maybe more.

She glanced at him. "I see. Like the soul; the energy can take so many forms. Then it freezes and crystallizes and becomes a mask of stone. Like being dead before you die. But there it's not viscous." She lifted her chin towards the lava. "Not too viscous."

"No. Etna is a wise giant. She expresses herself often; she does everything slowly. She's fluid. She's not viscous at all."

∞

The lovers had come down to the town and were sitting on the ter-race of a café. They held hands and were desperate. The terrace was empty except for two young couples drinking Coca-Cola from straws.

The man remembered how, out of season, in winter, in the café, a pianist dressed in a dark suit and with black greased-back hair sat at the piano in the corner and played old tunes – *Smoke Gets in Your Eyes*, *Autumn Leaves*, and *Dancing in the Dark*.

Now, in the sultry mid-summer heat, it was somehow as if those tunes, as if the pianist himself and the bright blue chill light of those ghostly faded winter afternoons were all around them – like a cold mist.

The man wondered why his love was not enough and why she was so hungry for more. And he knew she was right. His love was corrupt and limited, not pure and strong and primitive, not simple, not simple enough; he was corrupted by his imaginings; he was a prisoner, too, of his caution, his pride, his self-consciousness, his fear, and his need for control. "You are a coward," she said, sometimes it was affectionate, sometimes angry, sometimes despairing. Yes, she was whole. She was direct and primitive and absolute; she wanted – she needed – more than he could ever give her.

"Remember the couple that comes here every winter." She was looking at him with her gray-green eyes, her feline brilliance focused on him, alone in the world, bright and carnivorous, mica and gold.

"Yes." He remembered the couple. The woman was a blonde, Nordic-looking, handsome, tanned nut-brown, in her late forties, elegant and clearly very rich. The man was much younger, Latin, beautiful in a slightly effeminate way, with the showy carefully manicured dark beauty of a Mediterranean gigolo. While the woman sat reading *Le Monde* or the *Frankfurter Allgemeine Zeitung*, the young man, staring into space, held her free hand and did nothing. Every afternoon, for hours, they sat like that while the pianist played his sentimental tunes.

"She bought him."

"It looked like it."

"I would like to buy you."

He smiled. "You have."

"Kiss me."

It was a long hungry kiss. It tasted of Amaro Averna and fresh coffee and of salt and the smoke from the hills.

∞

The great man stopped in the middle of the narrow, cobblestoned street and pointed his cane at the young man. "You do know not what you are, young man. You are nothing. Now, you are nothing. You may become a butterfly, or a big heavy moth. Or you may remain a worm forever."

"Okay, stop it!" The assistant was standing with his fists on his hips like an angry policeman in an old-fashioned cartoon.

"Purely inchoate and larval. Unborn. An egg not yet hatched. That is what you are." The great man was staring fixedly, pointing his cane.

"Don't do this." The assistant stepped forward.

"It's all right," said the young man, his fists curled, his arms hanging limp by his sides. He looked down at the cobblestones, at the dust on the points of his shoes. When he got back to his hotel he would polish them.

"An egg." The great man stuck out his tongue. "You are an egg! You are an egg! You are an egg ..."

"You must excuse us." The assistant turned to the young man.

"Cluck, cluck, cluck. I'm the hen." The great man dropped his cane and started to flap his arms like wings. "I'm the hen that laid the egg. Squawk. Squawk. Squawk."

"Stop it!"

"I'm the mother hen. Squawk! Squawk! Squawk!"

"It's all right," said the young man. He was backing away.

"This happens sometimes."

"I guess I'd better go."

"Yes."

"Squawk, squawk! Cluck! Cluck! Cluck! Cock-a-doodle-doo!"

The young man walked away. He heard their voices echoing in the narrow alleyway.

"Squawk, squawk, squawk! Cluck, cluck, cluck ..."

"You should be ashamed of yourself."

There was a wail, as if from a small child crying.

"Now, now ... Don't cry! Don't cry! For God's sake don't cry!"

"Squawk! Squawk! Squawk!"

"Stop it!"

"I'm going to bawl my eyes out until I'm blind. Do you think the young man liked me? I so wanted him to like me!"

Their voices disappeared. The young man listened to his own footsteps. He kept walking until he came to the central piazza.

∞

The seismologist looked at the books on the bed, paperbacks – Henry James, a couple of novels, an Elmore Leonard paperback, a biography of Franklin Delano Roosevelt, a book on poker ... And newspapers – *The International Herald Tribune* and *Le Monde*. And a script, a movie script, lying open, its white pages and plastic binding catching the light, a cheap blue ball point pen, uncapped, lying on the open page.

"You read a lot," he said, as she came into the room. He saw now that she had lines around her eyes but she was as beautiful as the photographs promised, perhaps more so. "Eclectic," he said.

"Yes. These days my eyes get tired. Otherwise, I think I'd never sleep." She took him by the hand. "Some parts of me, I think, are voracious. Or is the word omnivorous?"

In the bathroom the shower was already on. "This was a good idea," she said. She slipped the bathrobe from her shoulders and stepped into the shower. She reached out and took his hand.

Gingerly, the seismologist stepped into the shower – hot water gushed down, splashing, and spraying. His body was tanned chocolate dark. Her body was creamy white, with a patina of gold from the sun. Intently, almost professionally, she began to soap his body, her hands ran down his chest, down his back. "You put a lot of vodka in that tonic," she said, without looking at him.

"I did," he said.

She looked up, reached up, cupped his face in her hands, and kissed him. He held her close, ran his hands down her back – the small of her back, the curve of her backside. Water and soap streamed down over them. Her eyes were bright with steam, eyelashes beaded with silver drops, eyes wide open, looking into his; her lips were cool, soft, wet. He held her pressed close to him – this woman who advertised perfumes and wines, whose face for years had been famous in the whole world. He had known her – hearing her voice, seeing her face, watching her walk, studying the way she raised a glass or held a cigarette – decades before he ever set eyes on her.

∞

Oh, God! The journalist hiccupped. He was alone. The ride in the cable car was a descent into hell. As the cabin swung up and out and then leaped off the launching platform, suddenly swaying free and hesitating in mid-air, his stomach plummeted, his heart plunged; bile rose in his throat, saliva raced to beat it down. He was going to throw up here and now, in the sparkling clean cabin; yes, he was going to get down on his knees and vomit, spewing filthy yellow bile everywhere.

He closed his eyes.

Vertigo flooded up, an irresistible impulse to throw himself out of the cabin, to dive down onto the vineyards, onto the rocks, and the pebbled fields, far below.

It was the void within him, into which he yearned to leap.

The cabin swayed, rocked, and rose dizzily to a pylon. Pausing an instant, it swayed gently back and forth, in limbo, in a vacuum. Far below were vineyards, rocks, and the sea. Then, suddenly leaping into space, the cabin plunged – into the dark.

He squeezed his eyes tight shut.

He couldn't jump: he knew that; the cabin doors were locked from the outside. But, still, the temptation was overwhelming, the gravitational pull, the yearning to leap, the dizzy suicidal lust, to plunge, to fall.

Oh God!

Down it went, the cabin, swaying smoothly now, down and down, down to the sea. If only he could keep his breathing steady, he might survive; then he could step out onto solid ground, kneel down and kiss the dust of God's own good earth.

∞

The young man walked down the main street in the little town – *Il Corso* – as almost all such streets are called in Italy.

He stopped in the central piazza – from here he could see, far away in the night sky, the string of lava burning, pulsating. In the central café, a man and a woman were kissing. The woman was beautiful, with the exaggerated, impossibly perfect, old-fashioned Italian type of beauty you saw in movies with Sophia Loren or Gina Lollobrigida.

The young man looked away and wondered what it would be like to have a woman as beautiful as that. It would be frightening. It would be too much. He wouldn't be able to bear it.

He stared at his shoes. He was imprisoned in glass, outside of everything, looking in. The man and woman whispered, their heads close together. They laughed and again they kissed.

The young man went to the parapet and leaned over. Far below, the sea was invisible, but he could feel it in the air; he could feel it everywhere. He glanced up.

In the Grand Hotel Palazzo San Domenico, lights were on in the suite of the famous French actress – it did look like it was her suite.

The young man wondered what she was doing. Perhaps she was giving a party.

The old familiar ache rose up inside. Why did everything happen to other people and not to him? He looked down. There was
nothing to be seen – but far below, invisible, the sea lapped at the
rocks and cliffs, slid over the sand of the beaches. Down there,
below the surface, the fish would be swimming, the crabs would be
scuttling sideways, the octopuses and eels swirling, the ...

∞

Terra ferma! So this was *terra firma* – the solid earth. It trem-
bled. Or perhaps he was the one doing the trembling? Somehow
the journalist – *no, fuck that, I'm a poet* – found himself standing,
unsteady and swaying, in the middle of the seaside road. *How did
I get here?*

The palm fronds glistened under the street lamps, lazy and
dusty, weirdly, promisingly, voluptuous. Out of the road's asphalt
intriguing patterns sprang up, epiphanies – constellations of pebbles and tar and sand – Yes! That looked like the Great Spiral Neb-
ula. Or perhaps it was Cassiopeia?

He turned around, studiously, to get a better look. No, it was a
Swastika. Adolf must have been here. How could he do that? Adolf
was dead, wasn't he? No need to go around doodling graffiti, sort of
"*Kilroy was here*" stuff. Already made his mark on history, hadn't
he? Why would Adolf bother ...?

The asphalt suddenly rose up and he found himself lying face
down, his nose in the pavement, feeling absolutely relaxed. The
asphalt was warm and comfortable and smelled of tar and rubber
and of long ago summers when, smooth-muscled and tanned, and
wearing only a pair of cutoff faded denim shorts, he had a summer
job laying sewer pipes, and – wiping the sweat from his eyes – he

would watch the blond girls race by in daddy's Cadillac convertible, dreaming that he might someday fuck those blond girls in the back seat, hot under the sun on the rich burgundy leather of daddy's Cadillac convertible, the rich bitches, but since he looked like a laborer, they had no eyes for him, no eyes at all ...

But this, his present prone relaxed position was not good, no, not good, lying face down his nose in the tar in the middle of the road. It was undignified. Someone might come along; or an Alfa Romeo at 150 kilometers an hour might arrive, zipping along the coastal road and squash him like a bug – splat, all over the radiator, or, more likely, smeared and tangled up dismembered and unrecognizable in the undercarriage ...

Spoil their fucking evening ... Or night. It was night, surely ... if the joyriders killed somebody ... a notice in the paper ... maybe a trial ... But wouldn't it be his fault – not their fault – if lying dead drunk face down in the middle of the road he happened to be splattered under their wheels like a bug?

He seemed to have lost his watch.

How had that happened?

On all fours, then suddenly – surprisingly – vertical on two legs and two feet, like a true sapiens biped, he managed to leave the asphalt behind. He rubbed his nose. The dusty palms, the curbstones, the small villas with their white stucco walls and tiled burnt sienna roofs – swayed. Then, suddenly, they were steady: Yes, they were steady – quite steady – unbelievably steady – and luminous and present, glowing with undeniable metaphysical glamor: *We are here*, they were saying, the palms, the curbstones, and the villas, *this is what is; there is no more, only this. What we are, is all there is; there is no more.* Fucking profound: the Being of Being, offering itself totally naked to him, directly: *What you see is what you get. No transcendence anywhere whatsoever! Or was everything transcendent, since only the moment was present, the moment must be eternity, must it not? And therefore ...*

An *epiphany*, that's what he was having, a fucking bloody tinsel-bright epiphany. That's what poets did – they had fucking bloody epiphanies – they didn't fuck around, the poets; no, they went straight through trivial immediate mundane presence and symbolic correlatives and all that fucking indirect impertinent shit to the fucking heart of things, right through to the transcendent *presence* of things without any need for the fucking ratiocination and the blah-blah-blah common mortals were so addicted to; they got right to the fucking point, the poets did, right to the fucking Logos. The Word! I am the Word! The Word is I! Or *me*? Fuck! *I or me?* Grammatical uncertainty is a bugger, a real affliction, *I or Me* that is the question. The copula ... what does the copula do, it copulates, it fornicates, it yokes together ...

But – Does God pay attention to grammar? Surely He has worthier things to worry about than the finer points of English syntax or copulation. Does God speak English at all? He remembered once having heard a Protestant Booby arguing that God spoke Greek, and another, better-informed New Age Protestant Booby arguing that God spoke Aramaic ... Who the fuck cared? These boobies got away with anything. I mean, a man's religion is sacred, right, and if it's sacred, you shouldn't criticize it, right, I mean, you might hurt the guy's fucking feelings, right, and so the boobies could believe and say any fucking stupid imbecile irresponsibly evil thing they wanted, and everybody would look sanctimonious and pitying and nobody would object, I mean if they wanted to infibulate girls, cut off the hands of thieves, stone the victims of rape to death, sell an AR-15 to a schizoid depressive teenager, seize the children of unwed mothers, or invade the bedroom of two queers fucking their fucking heads off in Dallas and haul them off – poor buggers – to some Texas dungeon, or blow up some fucking plane, or government building, I mean, it's their fucking right, I mean, it's their God-given right, the true believers believe, and belief is sacred, so whatever fucking thing you believe, however fucking stupid it is, you have an absolute right to ... do ... whatever ... the ... fucking ... hell you fucking want...

... the fucking ...

... the fucking ...

He was walking along the side of the road, tip-toe, carefully placing one foot after the other on the edge of the curb. *If I step on a crack I go to Hell, cross my heart and hope to die ... Eeny, meeny, miny, mo, catch a ... no, can't say that, can't even think it for God's sake ... what am I thinking ... and ... Once upon a time I was in love ... long time ago it was too ... with little Black Sambo, the melting butter and the umbrella were nice touches, and the kinky bush of hair and the Golliwog eyes, always did have a touch of jungle fever, just show me a nubile young black girl and I, well, I'd, well, I'd ...*

Ah! What was that? A lonely neon sign blinked, modestly, on a small roadside building – "*BAR*" it said. There were two little metal tables and some chairs outside, drably white under the lamplight. Might this Mecca be open?

He moved towards it ... the Promised Land ...

"A double whiskey, no ice, no water," he said.

She had serious eyes, the little girl behind the bar. She measured out the whiskey. "Thank you," he said. He went outside, sat down at one of the two little tables. He stared at the glass, at the amber liquid – like pure honey, like pure gold.

He took a sip ... Ah ...

Suddenly, as if by magic, the little girl was standing beside the table. She had on a skimpy tan-colored dress that was almost exactly the same color as her skin – dark brown. "Do you want peanuts? Americans like peanuts." She held out the peanuts.

"I'm not American," the journalist said.

"Oh." The little girl still held out the bowl of peanuts.

"Philosophically speaking, my dear, anybody could be anything, but that's not the point we're discussing here, peanuts or Americans, I mean, peanuts and Americans are mere epiphenomena, you see, mere tricky tickly colorful little bits of froth on the abyss of nothingness, mere bobbles and bubbles, illusory configurations of the manifold Maya, suds, ripples, and piddling whirlpools in the infinite phenomenal universe. At the heart of everything is nothing, you do see, my dear, you do see what I mean. So, being nothing, anything could be anything. This glass, say, with the whiskey in it – there's not much whiskey left by the way – it is nothing – an illusion. Understanding the nothingness of the glass, or of any other thing, in the world, such as peanuts or Americans or whiskey bottles, is essential; there is a Japanese school in Zen that has a word for this particular form of nothingness – That word is *mu*."

"Moo?"

"*Mu*."

"Moo." The little girl shifted on one foot. "Do you want the peanuts?"

He rounded his lips. "*Mu. Mu.* Not *Moo.* To completely understand this glass or any other thing you would have to understand the whole universe – the geology, the physics, the chemistry, and the cosmology, how the heavier elements, iron and so forth, were forged in the suns and supernovae, not to mention the whole history of life forms on the planet that brought forth the craftsman or industrialist who made the glass – but then, too, the glass is only a veil, a veil for, say, molecules and atoms; and the molecules and atoms are only configurations of protons and neutrons and electrons; and protons and neutrons are just configurations of quarks, and electrons are just ... but these too are only ideas, veils, Maya, illusion ... You see, my dear, if you don't understand everything

– absolutely everything! – you can't understand anything." He hiccupped. "Only God understands this glass, you do see, don't you?" He hiccupped again. "All the rest is, like the self itself, an illusion, a mere veil, and it's that illusory self that now asks you, my dear, for a refill."

"More whiskey? You want more?"

"Indeed. Double whiskey, no ice, no water."

"Whiskey. I know. I remember. I don't forget things." She put down the small bowl of peanuts, took his empty glass, and walked back into the bar.

He watched her go – smooth little-girl skin the texture of smooth brown butter, little shoulder blades like angel's wings, and a way of walking, toes pointing slightly outward, like a ballet dancer ... Ah, and yes, and she's just a lovely little thing, and that's the truth now, isn't it, with her dark hair up in a tight jaunty bouncing ponytail, and her slender little neck that could so easily be broken; and ... How old would she be? He hiccupped. He needed that drink fast – the more you drink, the more you need ... He hiccupped.

For a brief horrible instant he saw himself from outside – it was a true out-of-body-experience. From far away, from five meters perhaps, he saw himself, slouched in the café chair, his white suit rumpled and crumpled, his paunch pushing open his striped white-and-blue unbuttoned shirt, his sweat-stained panama hat stuck at a rakish improper angle, a parody. Who was this grotesque person he had become?

"Schopenhauer, my dear," he said, as the little girl reappeared and put the whiskey glass carefully into his cupped hand, "Schopenhauer says that all that we can know is appearance ... What was I saying?"

"Moo. You were telling me about Moo and that nothing exists not even the glass and the whiskey and peanuts and Americans."

"Ah, yes, Schopenhauer – the world is merely appearance, projections upon a screen, a theater of shadows, nothing but that, nothing really here at all!" He banged his fist on the table. The little girl started back.

"Sorry, sorry, my dear – but these things are important to understand when you're young, when you're starting out in life, when all is fresh before you, and when you have to learn your part ... How does it go ... ? Yes ...

All the world's a stage,
And all the men and women merely players;
They have their exits and their entrances ...

And ... Oh, fuck! You know what?"

"No, what?" The little girl stared at him.

"I've forgotten the rest of it ... "

"Of what?"

"The poem, the speech ... " The journalist wanted to cry; he was standing now, in a declamatory pose, as if on stage. When had he stood up, when had that happened?

The little girl stood absolutely still and watched him. She looked, he thought, like a statue cast in bronze, a Degas, with the lamplight golden on her skin, with her serious dark eyes, and dark eyebrows. Her lips parted; her teeth shone, white and bright. "My mummy says we're going to close soon. She says you should go home and get some sleep; she says you've been drinking too much."

"Yes, yes, indeed – your mummy is right." He pulled out his wallet, stood looking at it, puzzled, and staggered back to the table. He pushed some crumpled bills down, next to the empty whiskey glass – when the hell had he drunk the second glass? Empty already! Oh, time and its marvelous discontinuities, winged Time, so flighty, so quick, so capricious – Naughty Time! Peekaboo! A will-o'-the-wisp, truly. Time will be a 'fleeing! "That will be alright then," he said, with sudden assumed dignity and distance. He coughed, sneezed, and cleared his throat. "Well, goodbye, then. Adieu. Farewell. Auf Wiedersehen. Hasta la vista." He walked off, swerving slightly, now, once again, feeling very drunk.

"Goodbye," the little girl said; she watched him go.

He didn't look back.

Soon he was gone. "*Moo*," the little girl whispered, trying to remember something of what the funny man had talked about – whiskey glasses and Americans. She picked up the notes and counted. He'd left too much money, but, then, she supposed that's what he meant to do. Many strange people, when they came to the bar, and if she served them, left too much money.

She went inside; her mother took the money, counted it, and turned off the neon. The "*BAR*" sign flickered and faded; the door closed, and was locked.

The journalist was out in the street alone. No angels, no angels at all. He hiccupped. He looked back. The light of the bar was off – extinguished as if it had never been. The street was dark. No sign of the little girl; she would have forgotten him already – he suddenly regretted the solitary, egoistical, bachelor life he had led – Perhaps he should have had children, maybe a little girl just like that, a Degas in bronze, just beginning life, just learning all the new bright and horrible things that life has to offer, it would be like beginning again, beginning all over again ... just watching her grow, watching her become someone, a young woman, a student, then, perhaps, married, with her own children ... It would be like being immortal, having children ... *What fucking bullshit!*

Somehow he managed to stagger as far as his hotel entrance – and then entered. *Here I am! How did I do that?*

There was no one at the desk. He stood there swaying, and then took his key off the hook. He wandered down the stairs and corridors to his room. Several times he got lost. The place was a fucking labyrinth. He kept bumping into the walls and thought it was indeed strange; the walls kept leaping out at him, hitting his elbows, smashing into his forehead.

The hotel was an upside down hotel, built into the plunging cliff. The desk and entrance were on the top floor just off the old coastal road. The other floors – five of them – were layered underneath, cut into the rock, and going downwards, one by one, until they reached the terrace and the pool, and the pebbled beach that sloped into the sea.

Swaying, he stood in front of his door. His heart pounded. His head spun. Blotches of darkness scampered across his vision. He tried to put the key in the door. It jumped and spun out of his hands and dropped with a clatter on the floor. He stared down at it – a glittering silver triangular immanence on the dark red tiles – wondering for a moment what it was, where he was, who he was, what he was doing. He bent down somehow – blood rushing to his head, thundering in his ears – and picked up the key. With a trembling hand, and after several tries, he managed to shove it into the lock; he turned the key, and pushed the door open. He staggered into his room.

The room – bed, window, writing desk and carpet – all began to drift, slowly rotating, spinning, askew and afloat: the room dissolved and became mere color, pure form, an expressionist painting, a slash, slash, slash of the paintbrush. He tried to steady himself. Fucking killers, most of those fucking painters, look at Picasso! Fucking serial killer! Slash, slash, and slash! Cut, cut, cut! Look at de Kooning! Killing by proxy in pigment, the bastards! Chopping women up into triangles for fuck's sake! Serial killers, one and all! Shouldn't fucking well be allowed!

As the bright, drifting fragments of the room swirled around him, he swayed in the glowing center of the maelstrom, then threw down the key and picked up the bottle of whiskey he'd bought the day before – and holding it up high, he drank. The whiskey was room temperature. Sickening but invigorating. *Holy fire, burn me, burn my soul, burn my body, burn me to ash.* For a brief instant, a mere flash, part of his mind asked – why am I killing myself? *Why the fuck am I killing myself?*

He sat down on the edge of the bed. The room was stinking hot, no air-conditioning. It smelled of ozone and the sea, of smoke and the hills, of damp fresh laundry and stucco.

He licked his lips. "Yes, old man, why the hell are you killing yourself?"

Take care!

Fai attenzione!

That handsome fucking Italian bastard! "*Fai attenzione!* Don't do anything I wouldn't do!" Fuck them. Fucking Italians! Fucking stupid! *Fai attenzione!* Fuck them, Fuck them all. Fucking Italians!

He tilted the bottle. Whiskey dripped from his chin, staining his shirt. *Burn me, burn me to death, ignite me on the pyre, set my skin alight, I am your son, your daughter, your concubine, your spouse.*

He swallowed more whiskey, wiped his mouth with the back of his hand. Just walking talking scar tissue is what he was. A fucking burnt-out husk! Talk about beauty! Fuck!

He held the bottle out at arm's length and stared at it. My Muse! My Goddess! My only love and lover! He puckered his lips at the bottle, and kissed it, the warm, smooth, indifferent glass. My sweetie pie! My honey bun! Suddenly he had an image of himself, years before. He was still young. But the Goddess Booze ages you quickly, accelerates time, stretches it, warps it, and wraps it around you like a shroud.

There he was, young, muscular, tanned, walking up out of the water, his feet slipping and sliding on the pebbles, his body dripping with sea-water, warming with the sudden burst of sun.

In love he was, then, in love, and writing the best poems of his life, each word sparkled. And so he got drunk that night, yes, it must have been that night ...

Somehow it was never the same afterwards.

He drove the car off the road.

He sat in the car for a long time, listening to the sounds of the night – the cicadas, the crickets, and the stillness.

Nothing much happened. Nobody killed. Nobody hurt. Nothing had happened at all – the car a total wreck, but that was all: nothing, nothing, nothing.

Somehow he woke up from the dream that all things were possible. Woke up to life and didn't like it. It was a negative epiphany – nothing, just nothing, a spring broken somewhere, never to be fixed, never, never, never.

So now – now ...

Fuck them all! He lifted the bottle. The whiskey poured into his wide open mouth, gurgling and spilling over. What he needed now was a fuck, a good fuck.

He was burning. Everything about him was itchy, antsy, uneasy, bursting out, he could do anything – he was superman.

From the room next to his, he heard the click-click of a typewriter. The gossip columnist! Yes, she was already in the hotel, he'd seen her, he'd seen her at the desk, and then down on the terrace, climbing out of the water, wearing a tiny black string bikini, maybe she'd like to have a drink, she was young, she was pretty, she was more than pretty, she ... Maybe she'd like a drink.

A drink ... yes, a drink.

He felt like confessing, anything to anybody, he wanted to confess.

He wanted to fuck, to fuck and confess, to confess and fuck.

Take this prick, and say unto me ...

He was in front of her door. He knocked on the door. He didn't know how he'd made it to her door, but he was standing in front of it, carrying the bottle, and knocking, hard quick raps.

The door opened, just a crack, the chain holding it back, her face, framed in the door was tanned and her eyes and teeth bright. He'd forgotten how young and how pretty she was.

"Fuck you," he said.

"What?"

"Fuck, fuck, fuck you." He didn't know why he was saying this.

She laughed "*Sei ubriaco*. You're drunk. Why 'fuck me'? You don't mean that."

"No I mean fuck in general, fuck everything." He waved his arms. He began to sway. He lifted the bottle. Glug, glug, glug. "Though fucking *you* would be a pleasure." Glug, glug, glug. "The universe is one big fuck." He wiped his lips; he had intended to say *fuck up* but it seemed banal. The universe as one big act of coition seemed somehow more original than it being a simple big fat universal SNAFU. Perhaps like something found in Hindu mythology – the universe as an infinite onanistic uncoiling. And besides the word "up" had unpleasant connotations: chuck up, throw up, barf up ...

He felt the saliva rise, the bile rise, his stomach ripple, rotate and heave.

He tried to steady his dignity. He put one hand out toward a wall, any wall.

The corridor swung around, rotating quickly. His hand came to rest against the door-frame.

His breath was heavy. Who was this woman? He frowned: Bright eyes, oh, bright eyes!

"Look, you're drunk, you'd better go to bed. *Vai a letto, vai.*"

"I am drunk. I deserve to be drunk. I need to be drunk."

"Tomorrow I have to get up early. Be good, go to bed! Take an aspirin."

"Aspirin. Aspirin indeed. Fuck aspirin!"

"Get them to make you coffee."

"There's nobody. Nobody anywhere. Nobody nowhere." He began to dance – a jig – and almost fell down. "Can't make nothin from nothin, nuncle."

"Drinking's old-fashioned," she said in Italian. "You should stop."

"Old-fashioned. Never thought of that." He hiccupped.

"*Sia buono.* Be good. *Buona notte.* Good night."

"Listen!"

"Yes ... ?"

"I want to say ... I want to tell you ... There's something I wanted to say ... It's terribly important. But I've forgotten."

"You can sleep on it."

"It's the most important thing in the world – but, just think, I've forgotten what it is."

"*Sei ubriaco.*" Still she smiled. "You're drunk".

"I know, old-fashioned. Shouldn't do it. Betrays my age." He tipped the bottle up, drank and, lowering the bottle, wiped his mouth with the back of his hand.

"*Sia buono.* Be good. *Buona notte.* Good night." She smiled – an extra bright white smile, sensual lips, tanned skin – and the door closed on the smile.

Faced with the closed door he stood absolutely still, suddenly sobered, for an instant, perhaps. The corridor smelled like the sea, like a sauna, like a gymnasium, it smelled of naked bodies and sex and cast off bathing suits and old ozone and twine rope and tar.

"This is what makes me drunk, darling," he whispered, "the world makes me drunk, things make me drunk, smells make me drunk, there is too much of everything, a cornucopia, an abundance, an excess. *Be good, go to bed, take an aspirin,* he repeated, *you are drunk,* he said to himself, *you are drunk, you are very drunk, you need to be drunk."*

He turned away from the door. There was a painting at the end of the corridor; it was very significant. It overflowed with meaning. Swimming through the warm air, waving his notebook and the bottle of whiskey, he moved belligerently, head down, towards the painting. Into it, he would plunge, into the thick oil, abstract color, deep into the nothingness of oily slabs of white and black.

Oh, white and black

The wind in her hair blows back

Across the water, rippling, perfumes of her.

"Old-fashioned. Drinking is old-fashioned." He stared at the paint – white and black – as it swirled round and round.

∞

"So you know who I am."

"Who you are isn't important."

He kissed the crook of her arm, and ran his lips along the soft inside of her forearm to her wrist – blue veins in silken white skin – and slid his arm around her, down her shoulders, over the smooth shoulder blades, to her waist, and beyond. She held onto him.

"You are nothing now," he said. "Nothing." He kissed her.

His body was hard muscle; he entered her, and in her mind it echoed: It doesn't matter who you are, it doesn't matter who I am, who, I, am. She pressed herself against him. As she did so he entered deeper, twisting her back, lifting her up.

"Nothing." His lips pressed against hers. "You are nothing."

She shuddered and felt oh, yes, yes, yes, this is something, really, oh yes, and kissed him, then breathless, just held on to him, then her hands sculpting his face, and who, yes, who, no one, anyone, me, I, nameless, nothing ... Yes.

Woman now, man now, cunt, phallus, womb, nothing, everything, all, here, there, now, fused, now, womb, belly, vagina, shoulder blades, clitoris, breasts, nipples, hair, hands, fingers, sphincter, nothing ...

"Nothing, now," he said, "You are nothing."

Slave now, goddess now, child now, mother now, lover now, man now, and woman now, now, now, now ...

Nameless now ...

Transformed now ...

Nothing now ...

Nothing ...

She screamed and bit his shoulder to stop the scream and he pulled her hair, bending her head back, moving his lips along the exposed veins of her neck, moving, and the scream became a long sigh, and then a long run of whimpering cries, and laughter, and then a scream again, this time a real scream, a long rippling scream ...

∞

The journalist was outside on the terrace beside the pool, clutching his notebook in one hand, the bottle of whiskey, smooth under his thumb and palm and fingers, in the other. How did he get here? The air was hot. Everything was sticky.

"Fuck it!" He sat down heavily.

The smoke makes you drunk. He slouched forward. That's what makes you drunk, atavistic old smoky something or other. Sulfurous smells too, sometimes, like up on the volcano, like in the mud baths. It's like Hell itself, hot, thick, and viscous. *Oh, Hell!* Time speeds up. Then it slows down. The ideas come too fast to be thought. Then they don't come at all.

He put his notebook down on the table – ah, he still had it! – he hadn't noticed – the interview – years ago, the interview – with somebody famous – he tried to remember – a blonde and smelled of soap – he lifted the whiskey. Burning, it poured down his throat. Ready to gag, he swallowed. More like this, yes, more whiskey – that will steady the old nerves.

Oh, yes, she was French, the star, the famous, the world-famous star! Oh, she was so fucking fine, so fucking proud, showing off how fucking happy she was. The cunt! Icon of cool frigid Cartesian fucking Gallic cunt! Fuck her, the fucking cunt! She was showing off. She saw how fucking miserable he was, drunk already at whatever time in the evening it was, not late anyway, drunk already; she saw through him, so she fucking well paraded her – what the fuck do you call it? – oh, yeah – her fucking cool aplomb, *oh, is that lava?* she says, *oh, is that lava?* fucking cool cute aplomb, *oh, is that lava?* now that's a word, aplomb, cool aplomb, the fucking glacial ice cream ice queen cunt, lick my cool ice cream cone, you cunt, you fucking icy cool cunt, must be fucking fifty years old, I'd slash her, I'd cut her, I'd teach her – cunt, cunt, cunt!

He lifted the whiskey. It roared down his throat, bubbled over his chin, ran down his neck. *People like that, they never know, they never know ...*

His attention drifted. His mind went quiet, suddenly possessed by the stones of the terrace; by the quiet oily breathing of the sea; by the soft lapping of water against stone.

His head was silent.

It was silent and everything was rich and good and substantial. Peace reigned everywhere. The glinting stones, the oily breathing, the quiet lapping. He should go for a swim. A midnight swim. Right!

He lifted the whiskey.

He heard the click-clack of the girl's typewriter. The bitch was still writing, still working, he felt the anger rise in him, he half stood up, and then sat down again, heavily, and raised the bottle, dripping whiskey down his chest. He saw himself climbing onto her balcony, climbing into her room, ripping off her clothes, pushing her down onto the floor, her tanned butt, the white strip where the bikini left her skin untouched, the narrow blond bush – bet she has a blond bush, curly too I bet and neat as hell, a minimal fucking bikini bush, I'll fuck her, fuck, fuck, fuck, she'd like it, the bitch, he felt the blood rush, the erection harden ... That's what he'd do, he'd take the cunt, she'd love it. Slice into her like a knife into rancid butter.

Fuck it, fuck, fuck, fuck ... He drank.

He was old now. There was no denying it and no going back on it. Fucking a woman like that. Why, she could probably punch him out, beat him up! And where the fuck did he get the idea she'd like it? When did any fucking woman like fucking rape? Fuck it! She was young, good-looking, a hotshot glamorous successful Italian girl, and ambitious; he was old – well, he felt fucking old! Yes, he had a paunch that made him look pregnant, his teeth were going (some had already gone), he hadn't shaved in three days, he stank (rancid under the arms, he sniffed at himself), he was a failure, he ...

For some reason he suddenly remembered a hot summer day in Rome. It had been years ago. He was still feeling and looking young, and he was walking near the Pantheon and he met a beautiful young woman, a tourist. She was tall, slender, with black hair and chalk-white skin. He took her on a tour of Rome and he made up false stories about every monument they visited. *This is where Caesar died, Yeah, right here. He really did. Julius, old Julius. This is where Julius croaked.* Then he asked her if she knew who he was; she didn't; he told her his name; she still didn't know who he was. But I'm fucking famous, he said. I'm a poet. I mean I'm fucking famous! Really! She laughed. She laughed. Fucking fame! And she told him she'd known all his stories about the monuments were false, but she played along because he was ... because he was ... so sad. So sad, that's what she said, so sad.

She meant *pathetic*. She didn't say it, but she meant *pathetic*.

He took off his whiskey-soaked shirt and threw it on the ground. The sea was absolutely still. You could skip a coin off such water. He lifted the bottle and emptied it. He stepped out of his trousers. Now, fuck it, that's done, fuck it! It would be nice to take that woman, that gossip columnist – what was her name? – Gloria, yes, Gloria something – take her and fuck her here on the stones of the terrace, fuck her till she was dizzy, fuck her till she worshipped him, till she couldn't live without him. *Fuck it, fucking fantasy, fuck it!*

He lowered himself off the terrace into the sea. Lights from underwater lit him up. Awkwardly lifting one leg, then the other, he slipped out of his whiskey-soaked underpants. They floated up behind him. Naked now and not knowing what he was doing, he swam.

The water was so warm it was like forgiveness.

∞

The young man was handsome; but he didn't know it. He was very attractive to men, and to women too, but he didn't know that either.

You don't know what you are, said the great man. *You are a worm in a cocoon, you might emerge a beautiful butterfly. Or you might be a clumsy old moth. Ha, ha, ha. Squawk, squawk. Or maybe you're just a worm. Don't mind him. That's what they say! Don't mind him. Don't mind him – he'll never be anyone or anything. Don't mind him.*

The young man walked down the main street. He didn't feel like sleeping. He wished he had a woman to sleep with. He would feel better if he had a woman to sleep with. He could talk to her. They could make love and then they would sleep or maybe he would lie awake and listen to her breathing as she slept and he would feel safe and he would guard her and protect her. A woman's body would somehow compliment his body. It would anchor him. It would anchor him in flesh and blood and time and place. I am I. You are you. Our skins touch. He looked up at the sky. It was vague and black and there were no stars. Funny how sleeping next to a woman made him feel safe, he wondered if the women felt safe. What made him feel safe, what moved him, was that they trusted him – they fell asleep, those women he had known, they fell asleep alone in a room with that other animal they hardly knew and that animal was he – and inside him there was all the violence, all the dreams, all the strangeness, all the danger ...

He stopped in front of a shop window and looked at the display of antique photographs. There they were – the boys who were like girls. They had garlands in their hair, wistful smiles, and wonderful bright teeth. The photographs were old, sepia-colored, brown with age, blotched with time. It had been almost one hundred years ago. The boys had dark curly hair, smooth nut-brown skin, and big soulful eyes. They did look like girls, but they looked like boys too.

Perhaps he's a chrysalis. Not yet formed. Obscene, inchoate, larval.

The unexamined life is not worth living.

And the *examined* life? What the hell is that?

Can we ever know who or what we really are?

Do you want to be a naked boy being fucked by an old man?

Do you want to be an old man fucking a young boy?

Do you want to be a boy who is really a girl?

Do you want to be a girl who is really a boy?

Do you want to be a girl being fucked by an old man?

Do you want to be a young man fucking a girl? A boy? An old man? A woman?

What other possibilities were there? An old man fucking a young girl?

Do you want to be a girl – a woman – fucking a man? A boy? A woman? A girl? What costume do you want to wear? What carnival mask?

Fucking, fucking, fucking – a word like a cutting caress ...

Obscene, inchoate, larval.

Carnival, masquerade ... parody ...

The cafés were closed, the metal shutters pulled down and bolted shut, the corrugated iron stippled and striped with shadows from the street lamps. The air, dim with smoke, smelled like burning grass. The narrow street – *Il Corso* – filled with the smoky air, cut by lamplight, seemed longer than it was, curving away, hazy with depth.

When he got to his hotel, he took the key off its hook, and went up to his room. His job was to shepherd around the very important people – the French actress, the Italian director, the American playwright. He'd been a good shepherd. He undressed down to his underpants and went out onto the balcony.

Below, on the terrace, Alexandra and Giovanni – two of the people he worked with – were sitting in the dark at a table, drinking beer, and talking, slow, lazy talk.

Circles of candlelight on the terrace tables. Alexandra's blond hair; Giovanni was leaning forward, his white shirt bright in the dusky light.

"I don't want to," Alexandra's voice, soft, protesting.

"Why not?"

"It's too hot."

"That's not a reason."

"Come on, it's a very good ... "

Above the terrace, fifty kilometers away, the lava glowed: a coiled worm in the black starless sky. He went back into the room, took off his underpants and lay down on the bed.

He thought of the many thoughts he had had when lying in other beds, in other buildings, other countries, other times.

If you are everything, you are nothing; if you are everyone, you are no one.

He ran his fingers down his belly. He held the erection between two fingers, stroked it like an old friend. The underside of the penis is soft and silky and dry. The lips of the vagina too are soft, but quickly wet, or not so quickly, sometimes dry, powdery, wrinkled, afraid; sacred and hidden, those lips have to be pried open or gently caressed or kissed or licked open, to be adored or feared. The thoughts and images flowed over him like a river.

Alexandra's voice was a suave whisper. He could hear her, just barely hear her, like the suggestion of a breath, from very far away.

"No, I don't want to."

"Why?"

The night and the candles on the tables below made faint shifting patterns on the ceiling above his head.

He left Alexandra and Giovanni far behind. He changed. He slipped out of his skin, into other skins, he was without form, he was man, woman, child, animal, vegetable, mineral. He was larval, inchoate, he crawled in the primal slime, he sucked, bit and squirmed and wiggled, slipped slimy and formless over slimy formless surfaces of flesh, clawing, biting, sucking, tentacles swirling, breasts, vaginas, fingers, limbs, in the dark, formless, larval, inchoate.

The thoughts and images flowed over him like a moving tattoo, sculpting, coloring his flesh, mating his flesh with other flesh, all in the shadowy recesses of his mind, his eyes far away, emptied out. He was no longer he, no longer where he was; he was no longer anywhere in particular, no longer himself – whoever or whatever that might be.

Inchoate.

Larval.

Formless.

∞

The lovers separated at the railway station down by the shore. The buildings were square yellow-colored concrete. The geometric lines of the Fascist architecture and the long straight lines of track had been designed to rebuke the wild rocks, the cicadas, the hot smoky air, the vagaries of human passion, the frailties of the flesh, the wildness of semitropical nature: pushing – tentacular, tectonic, larval, and voracious.

But the Fascist rebuke had been hollowed out; there was no doubt what had won – the walls were crumbling, the once-modern station was tawdry and ancient, its architects long dead.

The man kissed the woman goodbye and she drove off, heading down the coastal road towards her husband and children. *He's a mouse,* she thought, *he's a rabbit, he has no courage, his passions are all burnt out.* She clocked 150 kilometers an hour. The road was narrow, cut into the side of a cliff. She laughed, picturing him as a rabbit – big bunny ears and a funny little furry bunny tail, his nose twitching hungrily. Oh, she did love him though, even if he was a coward. *All men were cowards.* The speedometer edged up to 180 kilometers. She turned on the radio. Dance music flooded the car, whipped out the open windows, into the night. *She loved him. She would never cease loving him.* The headlights lit up jagged rocks, sweeping past in a blur, 180 kilometers an hour.

Sweeping into a tunnel – at 180 kilometers an hour.

The man walked into the station and bought a ticket. The official behind the wicket was sleepy and unshaven. "Hot," said the official, his peaked cap was pushed up over his thick greasy black hair. His pasty white forehead glowed with dull sweat. He pushed the ticket through the wicket. In the bluish overhead light the official's stubble stood out like blackheads.

"Yes, hot." The man pocketed his change and walked out onto the empty platform. There was no one else, not a single person. The yellow light shone on the overhead electric wires that stretched away until you couldn't see them. He sat down on a white marble bench and hunched forward. He felt tired, soiled, unworthy. *He was a bunny rabbit. He had big long bunny ears, a little furry tail, and a damp twitchy rabbit nose.* He twitched his nose. The air smelled of smoke. Yes, he was a coward, unworthy of her, of what she expected of him. *Do you love me? How much do you love me? Why do you love me? What do you mean by love?*

You cannot love forever. No one can.

Even the most romantic, most passionate story ends.

Not even the most beautiful, most passionate, most intelligent woman can demand your soul. Your soul is not yours to give.

I have a life, he thought, I still have a life.

Something was breaking inside him. Something was ending. Was it only an ending, or was it a beginning too?

A breeze rose from the sea. It rattled the overhead wires, lifted a torn, soiled newspaper, stirred the smells of old urine, ancient coal dust, sweet tropical rot.

He stood up and stretched. The sweat on his back suddenly felt cool.

Love was dying; life was beginning.

His train was pulling into the station.

He didn't know why, but he smiled.

No one else was getting on this particular train.

He smiled, and climbed up into the sleeper.

The loss, the mourning, would come later.

∞

Naked, the great man looked at himself in the full-length mirror. The body was a ruin, but it had never amounted to much anyway. It was only his mind that attracted lovers, his mind, and then the money and the fame, and, then, well, then, perhaps in the end it was pity ... Nothing much else was left. What are we when we wear nothing, he thought, we are nobody, we are nothing ...

Zero, zilch, a hunk of naked meat – nothing. *Nothing can come from nothing, Nuncle.*

In abnegation, wisdom. Perhaps.

In nakedness, understanding. Maybe.

Tonight he didn't feel like anything. Perhaps if that young man had come home with him ... But no, the young man was an innocent; and that was the source of his charm ...

"Squawk, squawk, squawk," he said softly to the image in the mirror. "Cock-a-doodle-doo!" It was almost a whispered lament. Up close the face was a mottled ruin. It was a lunar landscape, made of pits and holes and rift valleys and veined deserts. The nose was bright, almost bulbous.

He stood back and examined the sagging paunch, the shrunken chest, the sparse white curls. Might as well die now, he thought, better than waiting for time to do it for me, my vanity dies harder than I do.

A breeze pushed open the bathroom window. It lifted the white muslin curtain and brought with it a whiff of the smoke from the hills – and the warm salt of the sea.

"Hell!" He leered at the leering old man. "Hell, I contain multitudes! I contain multitudes!" He grinned at the ruined body, the sagging flesh, the straggles of hair, the impotent half-hidden penis. But inside that body there was dancing, there were pipes and drums and violins, there were breezes moving in the forests, sun sparkling off the sea, there were tanned young boys, dancing girls, satyrs and nymphs, forests of desire, and words, words, words. He turned out the light. The image faded. He was in the dark. He was alone.

"Sidney!" he shouted. "Sidney!"

∞

It was very deep where he was.

But of course he couldn't see.

His breath was labored.

Moray eels, other creatures came out, hunted at night.

Suddenly, the journalist was afraid.

Maybe he'd drunk too much.

Suddenly the journalist was very afraid.

He tried to control his breathing.

He began to choke. He told himself he had to control his breathing, control his heartbeat, control his emotions – there is nothing the mind cannot do.

He choked; his mouth filled with water.

By now his arms were thrashing, splashing in the dark sea.

Oh God, I don't want to die, I don't want to die, I don't want to die, please, please, please. In full panic, his heart was sinking. Life for a moment was infinitely precious. Yes, that is life – infinitely precious.

For an instant, high above, through a rift of cloud, in the clearing sky, the moon shone, bright and resplendent, and suddenly, in a single instant, he saw all the splendor and all the beauty of the world he had known.

∞

"Michael?"

The actress lay absolutely still, listening to his breathing and listening to her own heart. His name was Michael, she knew that now. Since they'd made love that first time, only an hour ago, she'd drifted in and out of sleep.

Her arm was lying across his chest, and her fingers idly curled the hair of his chest, playing with it, touching the hard nipples, running her fingers along the collar-bone, down the tight muscular sides of his body. He was doing the same, silently, his hand moving on her, then resting on her skin, then moving again; he was taking possession, resting, taking possession, resting ...

"Michael ... "

"Yes?"

"Michael ... I like that ... Michael ... "

Sex – like a moment outside time.

I am nobody nowhere; no time no nothing ...

I am everything ...

∞

How did it happen?

He was dead.

The body of the journalist drifted farther along the cliff, entangled in seaweed, gently rocking, at peace now, drifting. Soon the fish would come. With cold snouts they would nudge, they would nibble.

The teeth tore his genitals. The testicles and penis were easily eaten, soft, odorous flesh ... It took only a few seconds. The dark water thrashed and swirled with blood, making a plop-plop-plop sound. The journalist's thighs and legs stirred and kicked and writhed lazily as if – without him – his limbs were trying to dance.

Then – sexless at last.

Snouts probing, the soft ocular cavity.

Snap, splash, implosion.

Heavily, the body rolled over, the sea was slowly rising, the body rolled over and over and then the face was upward, just out of the water.

Eyeless – at last.

Something reached out a snub-like snout, its sharp teeth bared. The scaly snout brushed against the journalist's lips – it was almost like a kiss – the journalist slowly rotated, floating gently, to meet the kiss, and the snout opened, and then – closed its razor-sharp teeth.

Tongueless – at last. No more speech, no more words, no more thoughts ...

The sky had begun to clear. Behind the ragged clouds you could see stars, a high immensity of stars, a scattering of constellations, and then, once again, the moon.

Like the whorl of iridescence in the eye of a dead fish, the water swirled. White and blind and striated with red, water and blood streamed over the mutilated face. The dark streamed away, like tears, cool silver in the light of the moon.

On the hotel terrace Gloria stood uncertain. She held the towel close. She wondered whether she should call for help. Perhaps he had just gone for a swim. Perhaps he was in his room sleeping.

She was typing when she thought she heard a cry.

Then nothing ...

So she came out to see.

His underpants were floating on the water.

His sandals were at the water's edge.

Pages fluttered, making a rippling sound.

Startled, Gloria turned. She realized she was trembling. On a table lay the journalist's spiral notebook.

She moved towards it and looked down – an interview, oh, yes, an interview with ... Gloria slipped her glasses down from her forehead and frowned. "*The truth is ...* "

"*The truth is ...* "

The wind rose. The pages fluttered. The words raced past. All the truths and all the lies flickered in the moonlight.

A faint, liberating breeze rose from the sea.

That was the Summer That…

THAT WAS THE SUMMER that everybody slept with everybody. Natasha broke up with her lover and she and I had lunch and got drunk together on white wine and cognac to console her and went to bed hungry for sex and sympathy in the shimmering golden afternoon and spent a steamy night which didn't even leave us with a hangover.

Since I was booked up – what with usually sleeping with Chloé – I introduced Natasha to a handsome exiled young filmmaker, thinking he might cheer her up and indeed she promptly went to bed with him and the next morning they headed off to a spa on an island off Naples and made love in the mud and under the palms in a giant pool of steamy sulfurous healing waters. After washing off the mud and swimming in the warm smoky twilight of the azure sea, they made love again, naked and alone, just the two of them, on the vast expanse of a big white powdery pebbled beach where everything was blood-red from the setting sun. "He was painted in bright red war paint," Natasha said, "and so was I."

As soon as she got back from the island mud baths, Natasha told me all of this, and she and I decided to get drunk in a river restaurant on a barge on the Tiber in the middle of Rome. We were the only customers. The waitress in an ultra-short emerald skirt and high-heeled black cork pumps brought bottle after bottle. My eyes were wide open, pupils dilated – ecstasy hovering, haloes forming, haloes dissolving. The tablecloths were bright blinding white. The gray water of the Tiber swirled slowly by – fertile and smoldering – like the pure mud that it was.

"Is fornication all there is? I mean, to life?" Natasha asked, raising a jet-black eyebrow. Her eyes were green. Freckles crossed the perfect bridge of her nose. "I don't know," I said, "is it?"

To squeeze some meaning and sense out of our lives, Natasha and I did some accounting. We reckoned up and compared the number of lovers we'd had. We totted up in columns our numerous fornications.

Who had had more fornications? That was the question. He or she who lost – losing meant having accomplished fewer fully-qualified, certified, authentic copulations – penetration was a sine qua non – would pay for the next bottle. Not surprisingly, I lost.

Then, turning our attention to comparative cultural anthropology, we listed our lovers by nationality – French, Australian, German, Russian, Somalian, Nigerian, Italian, Japanese, Sri Lankan, and etc. – and gave them scores from zero to five stars – like the *Guide Michelin* for food and monuments. One set of stars was for how good, or bad, the sex was. The other set of stars was for the quality of the conversation, the intimacy and beauty of the human side of the relationship, or its pure unadulterated creepy shivering unredeemable horror.

For Natasha, the correlation between the two sets of stars – sexual ecstasy and conversational delight – was generally negative; the better the sex, the more hideous the relationship; for me, with a few honorable exceptions, the correlation was positive, or seemingly so. The better the sex, the more it ended up that, somehow, mysteriously, I seemed to like my partner and she seemed to like me, though, frankly, when it comes to sex and friendships, I cheat and lie a lot.

We drew no particular conclusions from these contrasting correlations, but went back to my top floor apartment and – dropping our clothes on the way through the various rooms – we tiptoed out onto the terrace and made love on the colorful blue-and-yellow, sun-warmed Sicilian ceramic tiles bathed in the soothing unctuous glowing Roman rooftop twilight – like a slathering of golden olive oil – near a pot of bright geraniums that smelled acerbic and fecund and faintly bitter like mother earth herself.

Our friend Faustina took up the exiled young filmmaker, who – rather quickly in truth – had been dumped by Natasha. "He lacks finesse," Natasha had declared.

Faustina explained to the filmmaker that this, their experimental tryst, would be merely a temporary expedient for both of them since Faustina was already, in her spare time, the lover of a powerful politician – the Minister of the Interior in the Government – who happened, at that particular happy moment, to be away on holiday in Brazil with his wife and three children. The filmmaker was flattered that such an important woman who had such an important lover – Faustina was successful with or without the Minister of the Interior in the Government – would find the time, between appointments, to have sex with him.

After a meal of squid and oysters and white wine the filmmaker and Faustina fulfilled their amorous contract, so I was later told, and they did it in the shelter of a yellow-and-blue upturned wooden fishing boat covered in brown and crusty barnacles on a blanket on the beach. The sand cooled slowly but the air stayed warm. They watched the sun go down – the sunset was spectacular, said the filmmaker, then the stars came out, and a scattering of bright constellations declared themselves: Libra and Scorpius, Cassiopeia and Ursa Minor. They drove back to town and slept in Faustina's big soft downy bed, a strangely fluffy feminine bed for such a fiery vibrantly virile woman. So it seemed, at least, to the young filmmaker.

When Faustina's powerful politician came back to town, the exiled young filmmaker found himself tossed into the arms of Samantha whom I'd inadvertently introduced him to with the warning that he'd better watch out! Samantha was irresistible, I said. He might find himself hooked, I said, which, I told him, would not in the present order of things be a good idea since Samantha was also – at that time – capricious as a diva, changeable as the autumn mists, cyclical as the seasons, and inadvertently – operatically – cruel.

"Hysterics need to seduce, all the time," Samantha had informed me, expatiating on her own vagabond will-o'-the-wisp irresponsibly nomadic, inadvertently cruel, bohemian nature, which had left bodies, male and female, scattered all over the landscape. "I am a Classic Hysteric in the old Viennese Mode – a compulsive seductress. I get bored quickly. I crave – I *need* – the shivery tingle of a new conquest." Samantha, so people had told me, had been analyzed by a doctor in Paris called Lacan so she was supposed to know what she was talking about. "He had such skinny arms," she said of the great Doctor Lacan, "and he had elbows like lemon pips. I was afraid that when he made a grab for me – which he did, desperately, suddenly, as I was leaving at the end of our very last appointment – I was surprised his mouth was so soft – it was not unpleasant at all – I was afraid that, pushing him away, I might break him in half, which I almost did. He fell down and began to cry – like a teething baby – I felt guilty for a whole day."

The exiled young filmmaker took my warning to heart; he began the affair with Samantha with timorous and dark foreboding, knowing it was doomed and could not last. He and Samantha made love for two weeks. After the end, he told me what by report I already knew: That in love-making Samantha was as slippery and as muscular as an electric eel, as playful and inventive as a circus full of clowns, as lusciously smooth to enter as half-melted butter, as ironic as Socrates, as witty as Noel Coward, as, as, as ... The young filmmaker was waving his hands around in a Latin manner, groping for the right words. "I know," I said, "I know, I know, I know. Watch out," I said, "Watch out!"

When I'd inadvertently first introduced the young filmmaker to Samantha – this is a *flashback* – I had been dining with Samantha. We were at an intimate corner table inside my favorite bistro with two fluttering candles and eating arugula salad with parmesan cheese and we were trying to decide what to do with Samantha's most recent ex-lover, whom she'd kicked out the month before. He was very unhappy at being kicked out, and he was an aspiring melancholy novelist.

After Samantha kicked him out, the aspiring melancholy novelist had had a brief moment – less than a week – with Faustina. Faustina liked the aspiring novelist all right and allowed him to make love to her in her big fluffy bed which was full of bounce, but her dogs – two aristocratic Doberman Pinschers – didn't like this and then the young filmmaker came along whom the dogs liked much better; in fact, they licked his hands. "Why not get the melancholy novelist to try Natasha?" I said to Samantha and the moment I said this, the door of the restaurant opened, a waft of warm perfumed evening air, softly rippling, brushed over us, and the exiled young filmmaker – he was, unfortunately, devilishly handsome – came in and was thus inadvertently introduced to Samantha, which was the absolute opposite of my intention. Now I've done it, I muttered, now I've done it.

Following our advice, Natasha kindly decided to give the abandoned aspiring melancholy novelist a try and I said to her, "That will make one more on your score." "Yes," she said and took out our *Guide Michelin* list. "But the stars will have to wait," she said, biting her lip.

Seeing Chloé was out of town and everyone was occupied, I took up again with Paola, a petite golden-skinned journalist, and started visiting her in her flat in the outskirts of town and we went to the beach together and talked of Samantha and Natasha and Faustina. Out of the empty blue, the sun shone down. Out on the sand, women in topless reclined on canvas deck chairs reading *La Stampa* or *The International Herald Tribune* or played volley-ball in topless one-piece string-bikinis. Over a bottle of *Pino Grigio* and a plate of mussels, Paola, her big dark glasses tilted up on her severely pulled-back blond chignon, told me how she had once made love to Samantha ...

Cough ... "Really?" I said.

"Yes..." said Paola, and she told me in rigorous scientific detail how she had made love to Samantha.

Time skipped a heartbeat.

"Really," I repeated, envisaging this suave, tanned, multi-limbed sapphic pretzel. Let's see! I half closed my eyes. Geometry and trig-onometry I have always found offer a difficult challenge to the visual imagination. Let's see! I found it moderately exciting. No – much more than moderately, I found it extremely moderately exciting. One of the mysteries of male psychology is this: the fascination we men seem to have with the image of women making love to women. "I didn't know you two indulged in sapphic athletics," I said.

"Sapphic? What's sapphic about it? Two women making love – that's sapphic? It sounds pretty portentous or pretentious or com-plicated or classical or something." Paola blinked at me, eyebrows raised, a sunny twinkle reflecting in her irises.

"I think so," I said, "Sapphic. It's Greek. She was a poet, and ..."

"Words are just words," Paola grinned. She knew very well who Sappho was and what sapphic meant. She turned her attention, brow furrowed, to prying a stubborn mussel free from its shell, "What hap-pens is quite different from words. Words are inadequate. Language is a clumsy instrument. In any case, sometimes we do, Samantha and I, you know, yes, sometimes we do. In fact, several times we did."

Dreamily, she looked up, licked her lips, and closed her eyes. "Let's see, one rainy afternoon last winter in Padua; one – no, two – weekends in Paris; it was in the special corner room in that little hotel by the Jardin de Luxembourg, you know, the one you told me about; and once on that holiday, two years ago, in the spa, when we were all steamy in the shower, washing off the mud, on the Island of Ischia."

She blinked, as if waking from a dream, and asked me if I liked her new perfume. She held out her wrist; I sniffed. *Opium*: those were the days; in every airport I went through, I found myself lining up and shelling out and buying *Opium* for Chloé, for Paola, for Natasha, for Niki ...

This conversation was taking place under the rustling wooden palm frond-and-bamboo awning that partly shaded the flagstone terrace of our regular restaurant on the beach. The owner, Luigi, who had a droopy tobacco-stained blond handlebar mustache, a big wide-toothed smile, and sleepy eyes, and played amateur soccer, arrived with another bottle. He stood there and talked to us about his wife who, he said, was so jealous he wasn't even allowed to go out for a drink with the boys. He might even have to give up soccer. The wife, a handsome blonde with a languid long pale face and a ponytail down to her waist, came to join us since she saw Luigi was in a dangerously confiding mood. We were enthusiastically chipper and cheerfully talked to her, in great detail, about the weather, which was hot and, as usual, without a cloud in the sky.

∞

I later asked Samantha about her adventures with Paola and she laughed and said, "Yes, darling. Some of us do, some of us don't.

Some of us do some of the time; some of us do all of the time. Personally, I do, some of the time."

"Oh," I said, "Oh."

"Yes," Samantha said, "Men often really have no idea what a woman needs. Women are so sensitive. Women know – not always, but most of the time they know, they know just what a woman wants … no, what she *needs*, what a woman *needs*." Samantha tilted her head to one side and ran the tip of her tongue along her lips, moistening them, just slightly. Her dark eyes sparkled, and, of course, once again, I was in love.

∞

Since Faustina's politician and Minister of the Interior in the Government was back from Brazil, their regular siesta hour cavorting had resumed on a Persian rug, up on the fourth floor of the first-class five-star Hotel de Luxe, their bodies lit by the cool striped afternoon shadows of Venetian blinds; but Faustina, favoring the Minister with a particularly sweet and prolonged kiss, with her arms wrapped around his neck, declared that she'd like a younger man too for entertainment between sessions with the Minister of the Interior in the Government and, having received his Ministerial blessing, and determined and efficient as she was, she soon found a young, tanned, tousle-haired, broad-shouldered, blond surfer with blue eyes, a broken nose, a five o'clock shadow, and a delightfully crooked scar across one cheek, who rode a motorbike and wore tight black leather pants and a black leather vest over his naked chest and had a large tattoo. "He's relaxing," Faustina said, "He has no conversation whatsoever."

"But is it love?" I filled my glass.

"It's called fucking, darling," said Faustina, using a much more polite and polished Italian word. In these matters, the Latins have the advantage of suaveness, polished cynicism, time-worn tradition and Old World cliché, of words worn to absolute smoothness by libertine centuries and ennobled by their speakers' polymorphous pagan forefathers; the tongue of the Bard, alas, is, in this regard, a barbaric puritanical cold climate outlander which often falls short in matters copulative and corporeal. As she said it – the Italian equivalent of "fucking" – Faustina broke into a beatific smile, the sort of smile Giovanni Bellini knew all about when he painted all those Madonnas.

"Loving and fucking are not necessarily the same," she added, "not often, not for me." She paused, fingered her wine glass. "Hardly ever, for me," she said softly, and looked away, eyes half closed, to where the fresh green leaves were fluttering in the endless golden summer light.

Faustina's bike was bigger than her young lover's bike and some nights they would race, on an ancient empty road, just outside of town. Samantha and I took a bottle of wine and went and sat on the embankment of that old Roman road. It had been there for more than 2000 years, and had been built so that the Roman legions could march south and conquer stubborn tribes who lived in the mountains around Naples; it was lined with ruined pagan temples, an occasional tomb, a lone cypress here and there, and clusters of yellowish etiolated crushed used condoms on the crumpled flattened yellow grass. Beyond the road, along which chariots had raced and centurions had marched, empty flat fields stretched to the sea. To the south, the mountains, long-dead volcanos, hung in the fading evening light like dreamy shadows.

We watched in the dusk as they raced. "Faustina is lovely," said Samantha. "Yes," I said, clearing my throat. I was in love with them all, every single one, just as I was in love with the long crystal-clear blue days, the endless azure sea, and the golden haze on the horizon. The only sound in the yellow-gold dusk was the raucous coughing of the motors as the bikes revved up. Then the motors raced off, and trailed away in the distance, lower and lower, and then there was silence, and only the shallow sound of the soft breeze coming through the grass over the fields from the sea. Faustina and the young man both wore black leather but hers was sleeker and tighter than his, skin-tight and suave and worn as if she were wearing nothing at all – only this silk-smooth, black, burnished, second skin.

∞

One night the exiled young filmmaker, the aspiring melancholy novelist, and I, we had dinner in a small and crowded sidewalk café just off Piazza Navona and compared notes: We analyzed where we were at, at that particular moment in time, in the history of Western Civilization, and in the onward march of the Zeitgeist.

"Well," I explained, "I am sleeping with Paola, occasionally, and with Niki sometimes, but most often I am sleeping with Chloé."

"Chloé?" said the aspiring novelist. "Who's Chloé?"

"Ah, Chloé," I said, and I explained all about Chloé. "She is lovely," I said, "she's got these long legs, you see, and long smooth arms. She's lithe, overly cerebral, and very French. She is fanatically ideological, worships the sun, is deeply tanned all over and bent on saving the world, but confused about how to do it – wrong, in my humble opinion, would be more accurate. She's a Marxist-Leninist and Scientific Materialist of the old school. She is a marvelous housekeeper," I added, "a wonderful cook, and – in spite of adoring Lenin and Joseph Stalin and Mao Tse-Tung and Paul Pot – those guys murdered how many? – Maybe 100 million? Adolph Hitler was a hysterical amateur compared to them!"

I sighed, "Yes, in spite of all that, in spite of worshipping homicidal maniacs, she is an angel at heart, delicacy and kindness personified, with a flat full of adorable knickknacks, on every shelf they sit, staring at me, those adorable knickknacks."

"Like Heidegger," said the aspiring melancholy novelist, lighting his pipe, "You can be a Stalinist or a Nazi and still be a good cook." He half closed his eyes and puffed out a satisfied perfumed cloud.

"True," I said, "the relationship of art and life is complicated."

"Yes! Look at Eisenstein," said the handsome exiled young filmmaker, waving his arms, "Look at Riefenstahl, look at Vertov. Look at Polanski, look at Wells."

∞

At that time Chloé wasn't sleeping with anybody but me – she was too busy teaching two full summer courses – *Artisans and the Class Struggle in 19th Century Paris – Dialectical Materialism and Late Stage Imperialism* – at the University. Bursting with ideas, she smoked *Gauloises* and always wanted to talk all night. We'd eat late, in her tiny flat, get into her bed, and, lying sideways in the spoon position, watch the midnight striptease on illegal underground private Italian TV which was in black-and-white and full of static. The best one was a girl with short blond hair pretending to be a gladiator having her armor ripped off by the invisible paws of a non-existent off-screen lion. Clatter, clatter, the armor went falling off. The girl was cute and looked like she was batting at flies or mosquitoes or maybe a cobweb. In the end she'd be stark naked – except for her helmet – and take a small modest bow. A fanfare would accompany this and the image would fade into hissing snow. I'd try to fall asleep while Chloé, propped on one elbow and smoking one *Gauloises* after the other, talked at me, and – crossing her eyes in concentration – picked at the dark flakes of tobacco that occasionally stuck to her lips. She reported in detail on everything she had done and said during the day and on the meetings of her Communist Party Cell if there'd been one, and on how the class struggle and world revolution were advancing towards the final showdown, shoot-out, and world Armageddon. As I said, she was a hard-liner French Communist who also worked – in the splendid spirit of the Comintern and the Communist International – with the Italian Communist Party, while, as for me, I believed that, for better or for worse, Mrs. Margaret Thatcher and Ronald Reagan, like it or not, were the future. So Chloé unleashed the full force of the dialectic on me but I didn't reply. I didn't need to. I could snore. I knew Capitalism would win in the end.

∞

Natasha began to tell me – one day when we were once again drunk on our favorite barge restaurant down on the muddy Tiber – what it was like to make love in the mud. "Been there, done that," I said; and I told her about Lola and me in the mud, and Carmela and me in the mud, and Paola and me in the mud: Paola wanted an all-over mud massage at the outdoor warm springs in Saturnia – two hours north of the city – and I obliged. It was close to dusk. It should have been night. An eerie light, all amber and rose, drifted over the misty steaming sulfurous pool of the spa. The resulting erection was public and mildly embarrassing. Paola said it was cute and considered it a tribute.

"Did you put them all in the list?" Natasha wanted to know, "Lola and Carmela and Paola?" So I checked and sure enough I had forgotten one. "Five stars on both counts," I said. "Fibber! Liar!" said Natasha, "You are such a bull-shitter," she said, grinning. Her smile was glorious to see.

Talking to Natasha, and thinking of Paola naked and sculpted in a thin glowing glamorous gray sheen of mud, I stared at the reflections in my wine glass. Blinding loops of sunlight dazzled and teased my eyes. The sun danced on the swirling muddy river, a surface of churning slow silky clay heading sedately towards the sea. We drank more wine. Then, frowning in concentration, Natasha said we should put special symbols in our *International Fornication Guide,* symbols or little icons for, like, mud, or muscles, or dancing ability, tango, waltz, rumba, samba, married or single or bisexual or trans or cooking and ironing and pressing talent or Japanese flower arranging. I said I thought it might be too complicated but we should definitely think about it.

∞

Faustina's politician lover – the Minister of the Interior in the Government – was arrested for an important scandal – which was so complicated nobody could understand it – and ceased to be the Minister of the Interior in the Government. He was sent to prison and photographed in handcuffs, his hair all ruffled and his tie undone. He lost all his money. His wife filed for divorce and took the kids to America. His villa by the sea was repossessed by the bank and his Mercedes impounded. He was released from prison but nobody wanted to be seen with him. He was a pariah, an outcast, an untouchable, and, even worse, he was a loser, a nobody. Everybody turned their backs.

Faustina shrugged – "He's probably guilty, but so are they all! So fuck them! Fuck them all! Every single one!" She gave a diner for the disgraced politician in a fashionable Rome restaurant, out on the terrace, where everybody could see and the paparazzi could shoot and immortalize the event. The politician – only a few weeks before he had been one of the most powerful men in Italy – was morose, but he appreciated the gesture, and as the wine flowed he became quite expansive. "I'll be back on top soon," he said. We toasted to his health. Faustina smiled encouragingly and poured him more wine.

∞

Those were the days ... We spent long days, all day, talking and eating and drinking and sunning on the beach. We talked and talked. Was friendship more important than love? Were sexual desire and amorous passion one and the same thing? How many different kinds of desire and love and passion and friendship were there? Definitions and anecdotes rained down. And we talked about History – whether it had meaning and was going somewhere or had no meaning at all and was merely racing into the darkness and eternal night when the sun would consume the earth and the universe would freeze over or slumber its way into final total endless entropy. And we asked, if History did have a meaning, or teleology, what might that meaning, or entelechy, be? To cozy up to God, to drop in – in total submission – on Allah, to flirt with Yahweh, to attain Nirvana – or blissful self-annihilation – to bring about the Marxist Classless Society, or to keep on with the Capitalist Infinite Growth of the Gross Domestic Product and the exhaustion of the planet's resources? Or, perhaps, to promote the Maximum Intensity of Multiple Copulations and Orgasms? Or to make babies, to be fruitful and multiply like rabbits? Or to perpetuate, in Darwinian fashion, one's own DNA? Or, on the contrary, was the meaning of existence to create a "Life like Art" – a personal biography as beautiful & as elegantly intense as a Schubert Violin Sonata or as exquisitely balanced and sculpted as the frieze on a Grecian Urn? And how did the meaning of this Big Global History – whatever it was – relate to our own small, individual, briefly flickering, darkly-lit, tiny lives. The sun rose high. "Pour that suntan oil on me," said Paola. Her big dark glasses made her look like an insect. I poured the oil on her backside and smoothed it all over. "Rub it in," she said.

Samantha and Faustina and Niki and the exiled handsome film-maker discussed whether there was such a thing as absolute evil. Was evil merely what we disapproved of, or did it have some basis in the nature of being, with a hypothetical all-powerful patriarchal divinity dictating the laws? Was the ability to pardon raw and existential – an I-Thou confrontation between transcendent subjects, or merely legal and constitutional – or perhaps, then again, deeply, divinely, metaphysical?

Paola, half listening, lying on her stomach, turned a page of her book, Umberto Eco on the Semiology of Superman. The cover had a color print of Clark Kent divesting himself of himself to become Superman. Paola's backside and her back and shoulders glowed like gold.

We discussed racism. Niki said we were all racist, and that she herself – black and beautiful, cute as a button, and androgynous – was racist too. "We all hate and fear the other guy, whoever or whatever that other guy is. And we all desire and adore the other guy, whoever and whatever that other guy – or girl – is. And we all carry within ourselves all the others, all the guys and girls, as part of ourselves, all those hated, feared, adored, loathed, worshipped, guys and girls, whoever and whatever they are. I contain multitudes," Niki concluded, stretching, twisting her arms above her head.

"You're a poet and you don't know it," said Paola, looking up from her book and turning a page.

"I know it," said Niki.

The sea at that moment was a brilliant sharp blue with a white haze lingering at the horizon. "Could you scratch my back? And massage right there, on the nape of my neck," said Paola; the nape of her neck – curls of gold on satin honey amber. My fingers touched, my mind moved, my soul stirred. This is my religion, I thought. Here is my confessional. I pardon, you pardon, she pardons ... My hand moved over her silken skin like a prayer.

∞

When Natasha abandoned the aspiring melancholy novelist, Samantha took him back. Natasha explained that she had found him boring. He talked complicated stuff she was not at all interested in, and besides, she said, "He is too fastidious."

"Too fastidious?" I raised an eyebrow and popped an olive into my mouth.

"Too careful," Natasha said, "He's too fucking careful. He *thinks* before he does anything. He's always calculating the effect his moves will have – like, if he touches me here in just this way, will it make me wiggle my ass, or come in orgasmic pleasure, or sigh and cry out in joy, or have some sort of fucking ecstasy. It's like I was a fucking internal combustion engine or something, and he's a mechanic, up to his elbows in engine grease, fucking around with my fucking carburetor."

"Oh," I said. I swallowed the olive, "Oh," I said, again, "Oh." And I thought: Oh, I'd better be careful.

∞

Samantha said she would indeed take the aspiring melancholy novelist back; but only for a short while – and only because he was so sad. "He's suffering from block," Samantha said, "writer's block."

"Oh."

"Yes," said Samantha, gazing at me. "He says Natasha didn't stop talking and he wasn't interested in anything she said. So I said it might be interesting for him to listen for a change" – Saman- tha sucked at her straw – a quickly melting strawberry sorbet – as she said this and she added, "We were fucking at the time, me and the aspiring melancholy novelist I mean, and he was talking about Natasha talking while he and she, Natasha I mean, were fucking, which I didn't mind, even though he and I were fucking while he was telling me all this, about fucking Natasha, since, mostly, I wasn't talking, I was busy, concentrating, sucking and biting and licking, and thinking, rather dreamily, about his pectorals, which are quite fine – apparently he used to row – but, when my mouth was finally free, I told him that if he had listened to Natasha, at least from time to time, it might have given him some material. Because you know what I think?"

"No, what do you think?"

She slurped up some more strawberry sorbet, "I think his novels – his unpublished novels – all of his novels are unpublished – his novels are all so – what's the word? – It starts with 's'." She paused, then smiled. "Solipsistic – that's it!"

"*Solipsistic*," I thought– *solipsistic*. I'd better watch out, I thought. *Solipsistic*. I looked down at my ice cream: *Solipsistic*. I had already melted – into a puddle of pure vanilla.

∞

Samantha said that when Faustina gets up in the morning she is a flower. "She unfolds and opens up and blossoms like a flower," said Samantha. Samantha half closed her eyes when she said this. "Faustina's hair is all disheveled, her eyes are sleepy and fluttery, and she has that nice sweet milky smell of female sleep when she steps out from under the futon. Awake she's so strong, so dom- inant, but when she's half asleep she's a little girl. Her body is exquisite."

"So is yours, Samantha," I said.

"Mine's a dancer's body, all muscle." Samantha laughed and flexed a tanned, muscular leg.

∞

One afternoon Natasha got drunk with Niki on wine and vodka – it was a hot July afternoon – and she told Niki that she – Natasha – could only have an orgasm, if she imagined she was making love to a girl.

"To a black girl, like you," said Natasha.

"Oh?" said Niki, "to a black girl like me?"

Natasha leaned back against the wall. It was one of those stucco crumbling burnt sienna Roman walls up which matt green trellises crawl and thick leafy vines climb. The air was sticky. It was about to rain. The heat had built up to haze, then to cloud. There was the smell of rain and thunder in the air. "I mean, only if I imagine you, Niki, fucking me, or me fucking you, can I get a fucking orgasm," said Natasha. "It's fucking annoying." She leaned back and grinned at Niki, a silly grin of total drunken abandoned adoration.

"Well, I'll be fried!" said Niki. She grinned at Natasha, a sly, sideways, flattered grin. Niki was irresistible and her eyes were almond-shaped, yellow and gold, like the eyes of a sad wise old black man.

Heavy raindrops began to fall. At first there were only a few drops, then many drops, and then it was a deluge. They were under a restaurant terrace parasol, but the rain was bouncing up all around, splashing the table, splashing their legs.

"We're gonna get soaked," said Niki. She paid the bill, and took Natasha's arm. Natasha could hardly stand up. They went home to Natasha's place where they didn't turn on the lights – by now the city was sepia-dark with rain and thunderclouds – and they listened to the rain and thunder and darkness echo in the narrow streets and in the empty unlit rooms.

The melancholy aspiring novelist came by to pick up some tapes of Django Reinhardt he'd left behind when Natasha had expelled him from paradise. Natasha was being sick, on her knees in her panties – a string Brazilian black frilly lace tanga – in unlaced white running shoes in the bathroom without socks – vomiting into the toilet bowl. The windows of the bathroom were wide open to the beating rain.

Niki, her tight jeans astride Natasha's waist (*Giddyup, Little Pony, Giddyup, Little Pony, Giddyup!*), held Natasha's head – a glorious mass of jet-black curly hair now wet and plastered with sweat to Natasha's skull and her skin – peaches and cream and freckles – so Natasha wouldn't collapse and drown in her own vomit.

"Can I help?" Standing in the door to the bathroom the aspiring novelist rolled himself a cigarette.

"Make some tea," said Niki.

The aspiring melancholy novelist put lots of sugar in the tea, since he knew Natasha liked it that way – like Russian novelists, he thought – like Russian novelists with bad teeth and who drink sweet strong tea all day and who write big fat thousand-page books and win Nobel prizes. It must be her Russian blood, he thought. He waited to serve the tea while Niki shampooed and washed Natasha under the shower.

They put Natasha to bed, and Natasha sat there, feeling okay now, crisp white sheets up to her chin, drinking her tea primly from the edge of a big white mug.

Outside the hot rain poured down. It was night already and yellow shadows from the ornate wrought-iron street lamps made patterns on the dark burnt sienna walls.

∞

Daffy – Daffy was my doctor – was frightened: somebody was calling her in the middle of the night and making heavy obscene breathing and sucking sounds. She phoned me and I went and slept on her couch ready to answer the phone with heavy masculine outrage. *What the fuck you want you fucking pervert – I'll bash your fucking head in if I ... I'll strangle you, I'll pop your eyes out, I'll ...*

I was lying on the couch in the living room in the dark when Daffy dressed in a semi-transparent ankle-length white nightgown walked through the living room as if she were in a trance – or sleepwalking – and went out onto the terrace balcony to water the plants. The moon shone through the nightgown and on her shoulders. She was like a luminous shadow, a see-through illusion, a half-naked ghost. The watering can was big, oversized for such a slender girl. I got up and went out and sat on the balcony in a rocking chair and watched her water the plants.

She put down the can and held her arms out to the sky. It looked like she wanted to embrace the night – the moon, the stars, and the trees, the distant hills and the ghostly mountains.

"I love it all," she said, "I love everything."

Dropping her arms, she turned towards me. "Don't you?"

I thought for a moment. "Yes," I said.

Daffy was so petite and slender she often looked like a boy. "There are times – like right now," she said, "when I hardly exist. I mean there's no limit, everything comes into me, everything – the stars, the moon, the air, and the trees. Everything invades me. I'm not separate anymore. I don't exist. And, it's strange, but that's when I feel I most truly exist. It sounds silly. I don't know how to explain it." She was standing in the nightgown, her palms open to me, like a barefoot supplicant or a repentant choirboy.

"Yes," I said, "I understand, I think I understand."

Later – after a glass of wine – Daffy fell asleep like a child.

When the man phones, I tell him to fucking well leave my wife alone or I'll tear out his fucking eyes and eat his fucking heart and break all his fucking bones, one at a time, fucking bone by fucking bone. "You'll never walk again," I growled. The phone went click and when I held the receiver against my ear it buzzed the busy sound. I looked in on Daffy. She was still asleep, a slick of blond curls against her forehead, her face turned to one side, her mouth slightly open, breathing quietly. I went back and lay down on the couch and I thought about the night – and about how on such a night – warm and intimate as a lover's body – all the limits of skin and self dissolve. I watched the moonlight move slowly across the room lighting up first a sofa, then an easy chair, then an abstract painting – Joan Miró – and then the birds began to twitter, and already it was dawn.

∞

Faustina's politician friend shot himself, or that's what the police said. He went out into a recently plowed field – his shoes were clogged with mud – and sat on a log on the crest of a hill. He could just see the city of Rome and the plain leading to the sea. How long he sat there we don't know. Then he shot himself through the right temple. It was about four o'clock in the afternoon, a bright, cloudless summer day. The newspapers, typically, thought somebody had murdered him, the Vatican, or the Christian Democrats, or the Mafia, or the Masons, or the KGB, or the Jesuits, or the CIA – it was a plot, they said; he knew too much, they said; he was going to spill the beans, they said – but how, then, did the murderer walk across that muddy field without leaving a trace? Ah, that's what makes it so clever, they said, only the Vatican, the Christian Democrats, the Mafia, or the Masons, or the KGB, or the Jesuits, or the CIA would know how to do such a thing. We all thought the papers were right.

Faustina went to her politician's funeral, then to the cemetery.

She stood, elegant in black Armani and high heels, very erect, very proud, and alone. At a certain point, the widow – who had flown back from America – nodded at her – and Faustina nodded back. At the end of the service, the two young women, equally beautiful in impeccable black, kissed each other on both cheeks. For a long moment they held each other. There was a photograph in the newspapers, but no explanation, anywhere, of who Faustina might be, which was exactly, I thought, as it should be.

∞

Chloé and I have a crisis. I tell Chloé that I love the graceful stiletto-heeled way she walks. I love the bric-a-brac she collects. I love the way she perches her gold-rimmed glasses right at the end of her narrow pointed nose. I love the way her skin is tanned so dark she is blacker even than Niki. I love the way her long straight thick jet-black hair falls below her waist and swishes back and forth when she walks. I love her long sinuous awkward body. I love the way she pronounces certain words – with a touch of southern French lisp. I love the way her breasts are set so high and perky. I love rubbing suntan oil on her shoulder blades. I love the way she believes in the class struggle. I love the pedantic way she explains things to me, the situation in Nicaragua, the class struggle in the textile industry, the role of Finance Capital in late post-imperialist capitalism, or the subtleties of Marx's theories of alienation and surplus value, all of this expounded at delightful and interminable length. I love her cooking. *But* – I can't stand her talking at me at night – I need my sleep. Chloé begins to cry. Tears stream down her dark skin – perfect fine-textured glistening mahogany. She does nothing to stop them. She lets them flow. They drip from her nose and her chin. They make a silver net of snail lines snaking down between her naked breasts, perky chocolate

cupcakes, champagne glass perfect, and nipples as black as ripe
raisins.

"I can't stand this," I say, "stop crying." Chloé sniffles and
explains that what she says is what she is; that without words
she would be nothing; that mute, she would cease to be; that her
words are her; that the human subject itself is a linguistic con-
struct; that the dialectic of identity and gender depends upon
utterance, upon the Word, and is ...

"That's okay," I say, "talk," I say, "talk, talk, talk." She stares at me
and doesn't say a word but turns on her high heels and goes, naked,
clickety-clack, clickety-clack, into the kitchen. She was silent as we
ate and silent that night when we went to the movies. When we
got home, she didn't say a word, she just crawled on top of me, and
moved her body against mine, until I entered her and she moved
slower and slower and slower, sleepy and smooth, as if our two bodies had become one. We agreed next morning – negotiating the
deal in total silence and in writing as if we were two hostile sover-
eign countries engaged in an exchange of formal diplomatic notes
– that we would go for a trip on the weekend and we would not say
a word. Not a single word. Wordlessly, descending out of light into
darkness, we explored the dark humid underground tombs of the
Etruscans. Wordlessly, we walked in the bright sun, through the
blindingly brilliant brittle yellow grass, the cicadas ringing out their
romantic rasp-like buzzing, the heat raining down and clinging in
sticky sweat to our skin. Wordlessly, we pointed at things on menus,
wordlessly we twirled our hands at waiters. Wordlessly, we drank;
wordlessly, we slept. In Eden, we humans presumably had no words;
words are consciousness; consciousness is guilt; words are guilt. In
paradise, things come out of darkness; and to darkness they return.
The luminous instant is all there is; and it is eternal. It was like being
blind; in the silence, our perceptions were heightened and sharp-
ened. For us, it was a reprieve.

∞

Faustina declared that she intended never to fall in love. "If I fell in love, really fell in love," she said, "I would become a hopeless slave, a handmaiden, a servant, I'd be totally enslaved to love. But I shall be my own master as long as I live. My heart could be so easily enslaved, but I won't let it happen. Not ever." This was a challenge. We three men – the handsome exiled filmmaker, the aspiring melancholy novelist with the superb pectorals, and I – looked at each other. We were awe-struck. We raised our eyebrows. To reduce Faustina to a love slave! This Everest, we knew, none of us would ever climb, however much we might fantasize or desire it. Faustina looked at us, each in turn, and flashed that indulgent Giovanni Bellini Madonna smile which suited her so well. She knew we were pygmies.

∞

One night Natasha turned up with a new lover – an outsider, a Brazilian, whom she met on a supersonic Concorde flight or in a helicopter on top of the Pan Am Building in New York. "He's rather ... ah ... beautiful," she had warned us on the phone. She was calling from far away. There was static on the line. A week later, we were all having dinner on a terrace in a beautiful, small, intimate piazza when the beautiful lover finally arrived to be shown off to the group and get a collective stamp of approval. Faustina took one glance over her shoulder at the man and said, "Yes, he's definitely too handsome. I'm not even going to look at him. None of us should look at him. I'm not going to say a word to him. No man has a right to be so handsome." All through the dinner – there were at least sixteen people at the table – Faustina sat next to the handsome

Brazilian without once turning her head towards the fellow. He must have wondered what he had done. He kept blushing and casting timid glances at the impeccable icy profile sitting a mere few inches away.

Faustina was in a mischievous mood that night. She was wearing a patterned black silk semi-transparent moiré T-shirt, no bra, no stockings, high patent leather red heels, and a thin red rubber pleated mini skirt that flared out high up around her thighs. I was too much in love with her – I was in love with them all – to remain sober when I saw she was maybe – just maybe – a little drunk – and maybe, just maybe – a little available. So I drank too much, much too much. Faustina came home to my flat. Chloé was away in Paris for two days. Paola was sleeping with the head of a TV network, Niki was sleeping with a girlfriend, and Samantha was dancing – one of her own choreographies – in a festival in Austria.

In the midst of the piles of books and junk which comprised my furniture, Faustina and I danced in a cramped dark space to corny old music which was the only music I had – *Autumn Leaves, Smoke Gets in Your Eyes, You Do Something to Me.* I held Faustina close. She put her hand on my chest, curled her fingers in the hair, and said, in that deep voice she had, *I like hairy men.* I ran my hands up the back of her thighs to her ass. It was smooth, delicate, soft, an exquisitely sculptured and truly divine work of art. I was surprised at how delicate and fine a body was attached to that virile motorbike personality. I like smooth women, I thought. Under the sharp rubber pleats she was wearing a G-string. She smiled and next thing I knew she was pulling on her jacket. I stood with my arms limp by my sides. I must be too drunk, I thought. I always miss the boat, I thought. What an asshole I am, I thought. "Good night," she said, kissed me, held my face between her hands for a moment, and was gone. I danced alone: *Ain't Misbehavin.*

"*Well?*" said Natasha the next time we were getting drunk on the boat-restaurant on the Tiber. "I have nothing to report," I said. "You mean Faustina and you didn't ... ?" Natasha raised her eyebrows. Her jet-black hair gleamed gold in the reflected light of the river; her eyebrows were two dark birds in surprised flight; her gray-green eyes blinked like pools of sulfur. "I flunked," I said. "Oh, you poor helpless tearful dear old thing," said Natasha. Her full bright lips made a sensuously comic moue, and she ordered more wine. "Maybe you do tell the truth," she said, "Sometimes."

∞

That was the summer people believed in various things. Some terrorists shot people and kidnapped them and blew off their kneecaps and believed that this would overthrow the government, accelerate History, destroy Capitalism, and bring about the workers' paradise. Other terrorists blew up trains and banks, murdered with abandon and impunity, and believed this would slow History down or reverse it or stop it altogether, save Capitalism, restore true religion, destroy the Communists, and allow the rich to get richer, and richer, and richer, ever after. The exiled young filmmaker believed in making impossibly refined films. The aspiring melancholy novelist believed in the death of the novel and in his own writer's block and in feelings so subtle and deep they could never be spoken aloud or written down. Paola believed in lying in the sun, reading good books, telling funny jokes, collecting sexy lovers, and advancing her career to be the female anchor on the main evening TV news. Chloé believed in cooking, in friendship, in sunbathing nude, and in the Communist Revolution, which was going to come soon, and in the collapse of the American Empire, which would usher in the classless society and make everybody happy everywhere forever and ever. Natasha believed that if she made love to enough people, adding to our *International Fornication Guide*, adding to the lineup of five stars or zero stars, she would finally find the right love, the true love, the eternal love, five stars all the way, and begin to make babies. Niki believed that if she could only write the right poem and go to bed with a certain actress she would be happy forever after. She circled around the woman, and the woman circled around her. "She wants me too. I can feel it," said Niki, and I believe it was true. Daffy believed in working as a doctor for *Médecins Sans Frontières* – to save the dying and sick in some hopeless drought-devastated war-torn Third World Country and she believed in moments of ecstasy so intense they abolished her very sense of self, her very existence, her very being. "The nights are so beautiful," said Daffy. "Remember that night," she said. "Yes, I remember," I said. Faustina believed in style – Armani suits and dresses & black leather & moiré silk hung in rows for meters in her closets – and she believed in friendship and loyalty, in motorbikes, fast cars, good olive oil, good wine, good books, and her own courage and in her consulting and public relations business, which was more successful every day. And she believed in her own sense of *amore*: that love, which is not love, but chivalrous virile desire, heroic, principled, and respectful, whether it be a woman or a man who desires ...

Me? Maybe I didn't believe in anything. Maybe all the things I had believed in I'd ceased to believe in. Maybe I just believed in the beauty of them all, of all the golden lads and lasses, and the irrevocable passage of time which would kill us all, each and every one.

∞

Samantha's friend Rita was caught at the airport when some terrorists attacked the El-Al check-in. They used assault rifles and
grenades. Her body – somebody photographed her from directly
above, shooting straight down from the mezzanine floor I guess –
her body looked like she was posing for a fashion shoot. Her black
hair was spread out wide, like a wheel of dark fire, around her head.
Her eyes were closed. Her arms and legs looked like she was caught
running, or perhaps lying asleep, sprawled deliciously on her back,
advertising a particularly comfortable brand of mattress. It was
beautiful; there were no signs of blood.

A little girl, the eight-year-old daughter of an American diplomat, was
shot at the same time, through the head. We'd read it in the papers
but the father and mother retold the story to Samantha and me, outside, at lunch, in the country. *She didn't feel a thing*, said the father.
She didn't know what happened. He and his wife looked away, off
towards the horizon. He'd pushed their son, ten, to the floor. He
couldn't reach his daughter – not in time. The sun was shining bright
through the trees. Samantha put her hand on the wife's hand and
left it there. The breeze was hot. You could smell the resin from the
umbrella pines and, farther away, the bright haze and smell of the sea.

∞

That was the summer the magazine covers were full of the color red
– blood-red – and of the bodies that had been executed, bombed,
maimed, shot, dismembered.

At night, often, when we were drinking, gunshots echoed in the
streets and piazzas. Often all the steel shutters of all the shops were
pulled down. "Ghost town," said Samantha. We were walking alone,
in an empty street, late at night, nobody, not a single sign of life,

except for the bitter smell of teargas. "Yes, ghost town," I said. We came to a small square. We sat on the smooth stone lip of a fountain. Strings of teargas, like miniature clouds, hung in the motionless air. The water gurgled, soaked Samantha's dress, my jeans. "Ghosts," she said. She stood up, slipped out of her sandals, and began to dance, barefoot, on the cobblestones. She could do anything with her body. As she moved, her body rippled like the wind – it froze into stone, it hunched over, curled in on itself – an aged victim – it sprang into life – a lover, a goddess, a mother – it strutted – a dictator, military and metallic – a warrior, an executioner – it came up close: a face like a mask – a horrendous grimace of repulsion and desire – a medusa and a nymph – beautiful, innocent, and utterly terrifying.

She relaxed, dropped her arms to her sides. Suddenly she was Samantha again. "Ghosts," I said. Samantha laughed. She scooped up and splashed the water. We were both soaked. "Ghosts," we said, in unison, and for no reason at all we laughed again; and – the ghost of teargas stinging our eyes – we headed home.

∞

Chloé and I spent a couple of miserable days in London on one of my business trips. I was drinking too much; I was melancholy, and, with Chloé, I was impotent. We drove overnight to Paris. We got in just before dawn and climbed up to Chloé's old flat high up under the roof of a building on the Left Bank. The sun was coming up. We had breakfast. The rising sun shone through the windows. It lit up the crumbs and the marmalade and the croissants and the coffee urn. Chloé glanced at me from behind her *Libération*. "I think our relationship is over, don't you?" I was swallowing a buttered bun. I stared at her. "Is it?" I gulped. She sipped thoughtfully at her coffee. "Yes, I think it is," she said. "Well ..." I said. "It's not '*well*'," she said, "There's nothing '*well*' about it! It's not '*well*' at all." I didn't say anything. I drank my coffee, picked up the *Herald Tribune* and nursed my headache. Chloé was hiding behind her paper. But I saw that her eyes were wet. She turned the pages. The silence was – how do they put it? – Heavy. Yes, heavy. The silence – for a few minutes – was heavy. "So," she said, "Now that that is decided – what movie shall we see tonight? There's Bogart and Bacall: *To Have and Have Not.*" And so, after sleeping, chastely, all day, we went to the movies, in a narrow little Left Bank street, with the Bogart and Bacall and Howard Hawks crowd.

On our drive back to Italy, Chloé kept giving herself a low sultry voice, and, looking up from under her eyebrows, she growled – in English but with a French accent – "Anybody got a match?"

"You haven't got it quite right," I said. "Oh," she said, "Like this?" And she'd try again. "Anybody got a match?"

∞

I began to live my nights without Chloé. The summer grew hotter and hotter. I went to the beach alone. I stopped seeing people. I thought about my life, about what I was doing with it, or what I was not doing with it. I was my own boss and things were slow at the office. I wrote a few reports. I spent the long days swimming.

One day when I came back to my apartment, hot and salty from snorkeling, there was a letter in the mailbox. I took it out and glanced at it. The spindly black ballpoint writing of the address was familiar. I put the letter on a side table, poured myself a vodka, and stepped into a hot shower to clean away the salt and sand and suntan oil. I thought the letter was from my ex-girlfriend Susan. While I was in the shower I thought about Susan.

When I opened the letter, the gawky handwriting still looked just like Susan's. *"I understand you were a good friend of Susan's. She often spoke of you. I regret to inform you that ... "*

I poured myself another vodka. I went out onto the terrace. I looked at the geraniums. I looked at the tiled rooftops. I looked at the church spires. I looked up at the hot blue afternoon sky. I remembered long nights and days and endless walks and talks in London in the sixties. I remembered sitting in deck chairs on casually overgrown lawns, *The Times Literary Supplement* held loosely in one hand. I remembered long evenings in pubs, I remembered a tone of voice, the tilt of a head, a silly abashed grin, a quick gauche business-like, no nonsense way of walking. I remembered one windy warm afternoon lying on a hillside, on the grass – in Kensington Gardens I think it was – and we were kissing, and the wind whipping, cool and hot at the same time, around our kisses, between us, on our lips, in our mouths. I remembered vulnerability and bright humor. I remembered hurt glances she tried to hide. I remembered tears, just beginning, just being born, eyes glossy, refusing to cry. I remembered how Susan was bright with all the bright desperate hopes of that decade, organizing marches against the Vietnam War, making feminist speeches, printing pamphlets on nuclear disarmament. I remembered ...

Finally, I looked down at the letter. Susan had taken an overdose. She was dead

It was another country, and besides ...

It was July when she did it and I could see how she would have done it. It would have been a bright July day in that house in the little back street in Cambridge where she lived. I could see her going into the bathroom. Outside, in the hot summer brightness, the world would have seemed made for happiness: one long holiday. She stares at herself in the mirror. Susan has pale narrow green eyes that can hypnotize you. She has very white skin and lashes so black they seem painted on. She takes out the pills. She pours them into the palm of her hand: a pile of little round tablets. Outside she can hear the birds and kids playing next door and all the sounds of the vast summer day. The bright white curtains blow inwards, carrying the sounds and the sunlight and the blue shimmer of the sky. She swallows the pills slowly, thoughtfully; her gaze is now abstract, inward, absent, eyes that, already, no longer see. She stands in front of the mirror, but she is no longer there. She drinks some water.

Or was it whiskey or cognac? And she swallows some more pills. She walks back into the bedroom. The tall transparent curtains drift into the room; they carry with them all the muted shouts and bright light of day. She lies down on the big flat bed. Maybe she drinks some more whiskey or cognac. Maybe she just waits. Maybe she wonders, hoping, if someone will call. Or perhaps someone – who was to have been away for the weekend – will come back unexpectedly, open her door, and say, "Hello, what's this?" Maybe she hoped, maybe she didn't hope at all.

I went back inside and poured myself another vodka. Susan and I, it was old history now, decades old. The first time we met we had an argument – a passionate argument – those were the sixties after all – passionate belief and passionate argument were everywhere. Talk was endless. Ideas flooded in, throngs of ideas, bright, new, endless, burgeoning ideas. Utopia was so close you could touch it. We argued over a film by a French director, Agnès Varda – the film was called *Le Bonheur* – *Happiness*.

"Oh, yes, it is possible," Susan said, "it is possible ... Happiness is possible." "You didn't understand the film," I said, "the point of the film is the irony of trying to be happy, happiness is an illusion, happiness is always built on the suffering of others, the prerequisite of happiness is to forget, to forget the guilt, to forget the damage, to forget, to forget everything: to be happy you must be able to forget the victims, the dead, the wounded, the unloved, the lost ... Happiness is being obtuse."

"No, no, no," Susan said, "It is possible – the world is made for hope, for happiness."

Thinking about that first time, about that first passionate long argument, I went out onto the terrace and sat down. I drank the vodka slowly.

The evening sun was rich and hot on the brick and stone and on my skin. I wondered why I was not moved (but I was moved), I wondered why I was not crying (but I was crying). I drank the vodka and closed my eyes: And I saw her, still alive, still herself, still there – in my mind – still there for me when I wanted her – still there for me when I called her, still mine when I needed her.

We don't believe in death, not really; we don't believe in it at all – these gifts, these people who have died, they are never taken away, not really, not entirely. I got up and walked around the terrace.

The sky was a perfect blue, the deepening blue of a summer afternoon in Rome. I looked at the sky and I closed my eyes. I went inside and poured myself one more vodka. Time passed. Suddenly the sky was dark, the stars were coming out. I was drunk. I phoned Samantha. I don't know why, but I phoned Samantha.

Samantha took me out to have more drinks. We drank and we talked. You feel guilty? No, I don't feel guilty. You love her still? No, I don't, I didn't. I don't. I liked her, it was almost love, it was comfortable, she was a very ... how can I say it ... she was a very good person. She was very kind to me, she saved my life, maybe, a couple of times, she was ... she was my best friend, she was ... Oh fuck, goddamn it! Then, I did begin to cry; I did begin to cry, yes, really cry. "That's all right," Samantha said, holding me, "that's all right."

Samantha and I went for a drive. We drove late into the night. We talked; we talked; and we talked. Then we started to grapple. The car came to a stop, slung at an angle, across the cobblestones of the street, the turning signal blinking red.

We made love, we fucked, in her car. You, you, you, I said. You, you, you, she said. It will be okay, she said. I slid down her body, twisted her backward, I'll break you, I said. Break me, break me, break me, she said, come on, oh, wow, come on, break me. We snaked out of the car, down onto the cobblestones. We made love on the cobblestones.

Her body is swaying back and forth, her head is tossed back, her arms limply outstretched above her head on the cobblestones, her long black hair, loosened from the elastic bands, brushes back and forth on the cobblestones, her eyes brighter than stars and darker than night. *Yes, yes, yes, more, there, yes, please, there, oh, please, oh, oh, oh, oh, ohhhhhhhh!* And then it happened ...

I'm aware of nothing, only her lips, her eyes, and my hands on her. I'm hungry for all of her, to touch all of her, to know all of her. "Like this," she says, "Come like this, yes, like this, like this, like this ..."

"Slowly, slowly, slowly," says Samantha.

And then it happened – then it happened – again ...

"Now we've done it," I said. "Yes, now we've done it," said Samantha. We were sitting on the sand on the beach. It was dawn, almost dawn.

One result of that night, of that summer, was Robyn. So that was the summer that ...

∞

The next summer, Samantha slipped her T-shirt or tank top off one shoulder or opened her blouse and nursed Robyn anywhere – in restaurants, on the beach, in the car.

Samantha and I went to the beach one afternoon and we sat and watched the sun go down and the moon come up. Robyn gurgled and tried to reach for the moon. Chloé came along the beach and sat down and wiped her eyes – tears ran down her cheeks. Samantha handed Robyn to Chloé. Chloé took Robyn and cradled her and hummed a French lullaby. Niki and Natasha and Daffy had been dancing in a beach discotheque and came to join us and drink some wine. Faustina was racing her motorbike somewhere. Paola was in Argentina reporting on an international ecological conference for Italian TV.

The handsome young filmmaker turned up and moved around us, framing the girls with a square made out of two thumbs and two forefingers. He did imaginary close-ups of Robyn. Robyn gurgled, bubbles forming at her lips, chubby fingers reaching out. The aspiring melancholy novelist sat in the sand, his hands clasped around his knees, looking at the sea, which was only darkness.

Niki and Natasha held hands and leaned against each other. Niki was tanned so black the only thing visible was her smile. Natasha kept staring at Robyn. "*Someday ... *" she said, "*Someday ... *"

Daffy stood up and walked away, her arms spread, walking along the edge of the water, into the darkness, disappearing, saying, *The sea, the sea, the sea ...*

Samantha nursed Robyn and smiled dreamily. She was looking at us from far away. It was as if we were all disappearing down the wrong end of a telescope – and getting smaller, and smaller, and smaller, until we were gone.

Hi! I'm Back!

DURING THE FLIGHT he had put aside the scripts he should have read and he had a couple of drinks. He knew he shouldn't, but he had, just a couple.

Drinking made things so much more vivid, so much more present. This was dangerous. For a long time he hadn't wanted things to be vivid. Above all, he didn't want the past to be vivid and present, to be so tangible you could touch it.

He had one more drink.

The stewardess was attentive and friendly and had the bright eyes and fine skin of a young woman who has not yet flown too many miles or changed too many time zones. She had that intensity and high color that seem to get brighter and more vivid the more you drink. He had treated himself to two small bottles of Macon Rouge and three vodka tonics. After all, it was summer. He had a window seat and watched the clouds over the Alps and then, piled up on his right, over Sardinia. On the high peaks there was snow. It looked like snow. People are small things in this universe, he thought.

Drunks can be mystics too, which is one of the charms of drinking: drunkenness offers up insights ineffable and usually inexpressible once you are sober; but some inkling of transcendence, some memory, does remain.

A ghostly trace does remain.

Yes, of almost everything in life, some trace, some mark, some scar, always remains.

He asked the stewardess for another vodka tonic. He could feel the old energies, the old young randy maleness, the old desires, coming back.

As the plane came in to land he leaned forward. The empty beaches shone in the afternoon sunlight and the flat combers made cobalt and azure patterns in the shallow water, the lines of foam rolling, thin and white, over the pale yellow sand.

As he stepped out of the door of the Alitalia Caravelle, the sudden flush of the blindingly bright sultry heat after the cool rain and thin sunshine of Paris was like walking into a steamy tropical shower.

When he got to the old Volkswagen he'd left in the airport parking lot, he took off his suit and shirt and tie and shoes and socks and shoved it all into a paper bag and the paper bag into the trunk.

He stood on the parking lot asphalt for a moment in his underpants breathing in the asphalt heat, squinting against the glare. Then he pulled on a pair of faded frayed denim shorts, a paint-stained white T-shirt, and a pair of dusty leather sandals.

He closed his eyes and breathed in the air. The sun was hot and the air, drier now, smelled of salt. Yes, it was the smell of the sea; it was the smell of the past. He put on a battered sweat-stained straw hat and got into the Volkswagen. He was free – no work to do, no office to report to, no reportage calling him to somewhere at the ends of the earth.

It must have been the drink: He decided to go on a pilgrimage, to leave the present behind and to visit time past, lost time. With the afternoon westerly sun in his eyes, he drove to a small restaurant that looked out onto the beach and the sea. He wondered if the owner and waitresses would remember him. Five or six years ago he'd come every day and sat all afternoon drinking and staring at the water.

Two tattered gray bamboo fences began at the partially glassed-in terrace and went down almost to the water and marked the limits of the restaurant's territory. The bamboo stalks of the fences were split in many places and frayed at the ends and framed the beach and the sea. Between the fences, the sea seemed to hang against the sky: it was a pale, narrow, and slightly crooked picture, like an abstract, inexpertly hung, painting.

He sat on the beach in a deckchair and drank a bottle of white wine and watched the sun go down. Nothing much happens when the sun goes down but it is interesting to watch all the same. The waves of the sea were tiny and choppy, and broke the sun into a thousand sparkles that filled his eyes.

There were no people. The world was his and his alone.

The old owners of the restaurant had sold out, he discovered, and were gone and the barman was new so he didn't have to talk to the man or mention old times. As far as the barman was concerned, he was just a stranger who'd come to sit alone and drink a bottle of white wine and watch the sun go down. It was a weekday and the stranger was the only customer.

Down on the beach, the stranger lowered his straw hat. The sun broke into red chunks in the square interstices of straw and fragments flickered against the frayed straw brim. The sun-warmed straw smelled golden, like a harvest, like hay and straw, like an ancient, sunlit, wicker rocking-chair, veranda, and indolent afternoon. Like a secret childhood he had perhaps lived, and perhaps not.

He lifted the hat and stared at the sun. If you stare long enough at the sun – even at the setting sun – you will go blind.

He held the cool bottle by the neck and drank straight from the slippery lip, putting the bottle back down to rest from time to time so that its bottom dragged on the sand, and then lifting it again, but never letting go.

When he finished the bottle the sun was almost touching the horizon so he left the empty bottle standing crooked in the sand and got up out of the deckchair and walked down to the edge of the water. The water was warm and lapped around his feet. He took off his sandals and left them at the foamy edge where the water tugged at them gently.

He looked right and left, north and south, up and down the coast – everything was unpeopled – not a single person, just empty space in the powdery light of the low sun; the pale golden beach stretched away, and the empty, shattered, deepening sea.

He walked north along the beach for five minutes until he saw a big piece of driftwood – the trunk and roots of a tree. It was high up on the beach where the dunes and the long yellow drifting grass began. He walked to the piece of driftwood and sat down. Under his hand the wood was white and dry and hard and worn smooth as old bone. He sat on the fallen column of driftwood and squinted at the setting sun.

To his right, between the driftwood and the sea, a woman he hadn't noticed before was kneeling in the sand. The woman had gathered a small pile of twigs, of branches, and a few chopped up logs. She had two young children with her, a girl and a boy. A red kerchief held up the woman's pinned-back blond hair but the hair spilled out over her forehead. Impatiently she brushed at the strands with the back of her hand. He watched the woman and then he watched the sun and then he watched the woman again. She was barefoot and she wore frayed jeans shorts and a white blouse. She put down some tightly rolled up pieces of newspaper, then she put kindling on the newspaper, then bundled sticks, and finally she stacked three logs.

The little girl walked away, picked up a blue plastic pail and walked back.

The little boy watched the woman carefully. He put his finger in his mouth.

The woman adjusted the logs again and sat back. On her wrist she wore a watch that glittered like gold.

He looked away at the sun and when he looked back at the woman the fire was lit. The woman squatted on the balls of her feet and gazed into the fire.

The fire lit her up as if she were on stage.

Her legs were brown with the sun and her face was deeply tanned. Her blond hair had been bleached by the sun, and stained straw-dark in streaks by the salt. He lowered the brim of his hat and squinted, watching her.

The sun sat for a minute on the horizon and then began to collapse and break apart with dark lines running across it like the ribs of a giant rib-cage and then it broke into angry drifting dull chunks of red – and suddenly it was gone. For a moment, the sky was red; then pale yellow; then a fringed suggestion of pale green; then a darker blue, and finally inky black. Then there were stars.

When the sun was gone, the fire and the woman and her children made an isolated bright spot on the beach. He breathed in the perfume of burning pine and cedar. The sea, behind the fire-lit family, held the light longer than the sand. He glanced back. Behind him the land and bush and fields were deep in night. The fire crackled. Red sparks flew up. The children had high voices and laughed and the woman replied in a low voice he could just hear but he could not make out the words. Now on her knees and closer to the fire, the woman reached up and in one graceful movement undid the kerchief and shook out her hair, which was thick and straight, almost to her shoulders, and burnished like old copper. She had a thin serious face and high cheekbones and brown eyes.

He watched as the woman took marshmallows from a plastic bag and stuck them on the end of long thin wooden sticks and gave the sticks to the two children. They toasted the marshmallows over the

fire and the children drank Coca-Cola from tins and laughed and
waved the tins in the air. The woman drank white wine from a glass.
She laughed and showed her teeth and hugged the little girl and
the little boy.

She was a handsome woman and he could see in the light
of the fire that her tanned arms were fine-boned, muscled, and
strong.

It was dark when the woman doused the fire with sand and a
bucket of water from the sea. She and the two children walked up to
a row of cottages that stood back from the sea, with only their rooftops and some windows showing above the high dunes and the long
grass and low scrub.

He swiveled around on the piece of driftwood and watched the
lights go on in the cottage.

Now he knew where the woman lived with the two children.

All the other cottages on the small street were dark. It was far
beyond the end of the season and the other cottages were empty.
The woman and her children were alone at the end of the sandy
street where the street lamps shone on tuffs of dried grass, on shuttered windows, on walls with broken bottles and barbed wire on top,
and on green municipal garbage bins.

He walked up from the beach and squatted on the crest of a dune
and watched. A light went on, and then another, and then a light
went off. The two children must be in bed.

Parked beside the cottage was a white and very dusty Land
Rover. The woman stood for a moment in the kitchen, framed in a
window, then turned out the kitchen light and moved into another
room. She lit a floor lamp and sat down.

From the angle of her head and the way the light fell he could tell
she was reading. For a long time he squatted on the dune, watching her; and for a long time the woman sat immobile, her head
inclined, framed in the window. From time to time she reached up

to brush back her hair. In the lamplight, it was burnished, newly spun gold.

His battered Volkswagen sat alone in the cool circle of light of a street lamp. Giant moths circled awkwardly around the street lamp and a single bat swooped in gracefully to harvest the moths. The moths fluttered and banged against the lamp with a heavy ping-ping-ping sound and cast dancing pale shadows on the sandy oil-stained asphalt. The bat, as it swooped in, didn't bang against anything, and didn't make any sound at all.

He rolled down the windows to let out the heat of day.

The motor rattled into life, a shocking intrusion into the silence; it coughed, belched, and finally settled down. The bat swung in graceful loops and the moths continued to flutter, as if they had heard nothing at all.

He drove out of the village and along the flat dirt country roads. With the windows open the wind rippled against his face and he could smell the damp hot cooling fields. The headlights made a narrow bright tunnel between tall banks of grass and leaning yellow stalks of bamboo. He took deep breaths and closed his eyes, trusting the road to be straight.

The house he had rented was isolated in the country not far from the coast and stood beside a grassy, slow-moving canal. Mussolini had ordered these houses and canals built in the 1930s when the land was drained and reclaimed and settled with peasants from the Veneto Region. Even now many of the locals spoke with a dialect and accent from across the mountains, hundreds of kilometers to the north.

All of the rooms were empty and all of the windows were open. No lights shone. The vegetation, even at the end of the season, was almost tropical – luxuriant and waxy, with tendrils, heavy smells, glossy leaves and subtle poisons; the perfumes invaded the empty, unfurnished rooms.

He got a beer out of the fridge and left all the lights off.

The water in the canal was calm and pure black and a few stars sat in the water as easily as in the night sky. Under his bare feet the tiles of the terrace were smooth and cool. He pulled off his clothes and sat naked in the canvas and wood deckchair and stared at the water. The frogs made a noise from time to time and the crickets. Otherwise there was silence, though there is no such thing as silence as over the years the sound technicians had taught him. Every space has its own sound, they said, even the sound of emptiness. For every scene and every setting they always recorded it carefully – the "room tone" – the sound of emptiness, of absence.

He went back to the house and got another beer. In the living room he stopped and struck a match and lit a candle in front of the photograph. The woman had been twenty-seven when it was taken. She was now thirteen hours and nine time zones away and probably would be ... He glanced at his watch.

The sun would be shining.

She would be ...

Eight years ago they had rented this same house on the canal together. The house hadn't changed; it was exactly the same.

The candle in front of the photograph flickered, though there was no breeze.

He picked up the beer and went back out to the deckchair at the edge of the canal. The frogs started up as if on cue; then they stopped again. He lifted the can to his lips and drank the beer slowly. It had been eight years and she'd not changed a bit so far as he knew.

But what did he know?

She liked walking barefoot on the cool ceramic tiles. In the house or on the terrace and edge of the canal she often walked around naked, treating her long white body and its startling elongated beauty casually, as if it meant nothing. Often she wore a long robe, brown and black, like a Bedouin, and sat silent for hours holding his hand or curled up, her eyes half-closed, reading a book, or drowsing.

"Hi!" she would suddenly say, coming awake with a big grin, and stand up and rub her eyes with her knuckles, and drift into the house to make coffee or bring out another book or just to drift, looking at her paintings possibly, or stopping in front of the easel to work something out, touch something up. In those days the empty old squared-off 1930s farmhouse was filled with sunlight.

"Hi!" The sound of her voice echoed in his mind, from long ago and far away. There is no such thing, he thought, as silence.

They'd stayed through the winter.

The constellation Orion came up in winter nights, over the canal.

In January and February in the first hours of the evenings Orion was reflected in the canal. He wondered if it would always be so. He had tried to explain the constellations to her and the geology of the earth, but she did not seem interested in the stars.

Perhaps in centuries to come the sea would cover the land. Or the sea would retreat, the canals dry up, the vegetation die, and the desert return. Or an ice age would come, more terrible than any before, and snow would fall, thick and silent, forever and forever, and glaciers would build up immense walls of ice and scrape the planet down to pure sterile granite.

Or perhaps the earth itself would be gone; there would be no one and nothing here to construe a constellation out of a random assemblage of stars.

She had been here eight years ago.

"Hi!" she would say, brightly.

Who says time is real?

Who says the past is dead.

Somewhere around midnight he changed from beer to iced vodka. He put a squeeze of lemon in the vodka.

The candle still flickered in front of the photograph. It was in black and white. Her slender neck, full lips, high cheekbones, deep gray eyes, high forehead, and slicked-back jet-black hair oscillated, shadows moving, as if alive. Nodding his head in greeting he walked out onto the terrace.

He looked up: Andromeda was there: its two lines of stars sweeping down to the great square of Pegasus. Cassiopeia, a vast W-shape, rotated around the pole star. It was autumn, a time of endings. Soon Orion, the winter constellation, would return. But tonight, he thought, it was suddenly summer, as hot as mid-summer, the air hanging still and heavy, almost unbreathable.

That winter they lay bundled up on the deckchairs and he explained. "That is Betelgeuse," he said, "See, there, Betelgeuse is Orion's right shoulder, since he's facing us. It's a reddish color. Do you see it? It is two-hundred-and-forty-two light years away. And see the sword, the sword of Orion, dangling ... "

"Uh, uh," she said softly, and he could see her sleepy smile in the dim light of the stars: the whites of her eyes, the dark arcs of her eyebrows.

She reached over to make sure his shirt was buttoned up, tucked the blanket high around his neck.

"I like the cold air," she said, "Tonight we will leave all the windows open."

Lots of covers; clinging close; their breath mingling.

Touch, touch, touch.

Lips ...

He wondered why it hadn't worked.

He wondered if anything would ever work again.

Drinking, he would become maudlin. He was already maudlin, damn it! He would think about her; and he would think about the others; he would make up stories in his head. He didn't want to become maudlin. He didn't want to think or feel anything. He wanted that clarity of mind and of vision that came from feeling nothing, thinking nothing, believing nothing. If your mind is emptied out, if you cease to exist, if you are no longer anyone in particular, but everything in general, you can for a time see things more clearly than is humanly possible, or almost. It is as if you are a transparent sheet of glass; it is a state, of abnegation and abjection, he thought, close to mystical sainthood, close to madness; of course, strictly speaking, it is an impossible state – the view from nowhere is nowhere.

"Betel ... How do you pronounce it?" she asked, one night towards the end. She was holding two paint brushes in her fist and standing, her back to him, perplexed, her legs wide apart, thinking, facing a very large painting she had propped against the wall.

He thought about the tanned woman on the beach, so self-contained, lighting her fire. Her two children were her world and for them she was the world; later, there she was again, framed in a window, reading alone, self-contained, in the sudden solitude and coolness of the evening.

Crickets, cicadas.

The lapping of waves.

He would like to know her, he thought; then he checked the thought as being typically maudlin. He was imagining an adventure, a new form of companionship, of love; it was a ridiculous tawdry romantic drunkard's fantasy; as a man, he was absolutely pathetic.

He thought of the Alitalia stewardess. She was – or seemed – so bright, so untarnished. What sort of life did she have? Married, single, living with a lover? Was she sleeping in Rome tonight, or in Paris? Did she read books or ...

The vodka was talking.

It didn't matter. Nothing would happen; and, whatever

happened would be the same as what had happened before. He had reached that time of life when you realize nothing new will ever happen again because you now finally know who you are and what you are and where your limits lie and that there is no hope or health in you.

Yes, he was being maudlin.

Definitely!

What a jerk!

He went back to the refrigerator and poured himself another vodka. This time he didn't bother with the squeeze of lemon. In front of the photograph the candle still flickered, by now burnt almost to a smudged stub. He knew his way in the dark and moved without needing to think about it out onto the terrace. A bullfrog croaked, croaked again, and fell silent. Something splashed in the canal, and ripples disturbed the reflected stars: some small animal, swimming from one bank to the other.

She would not paint for many days. Then suddenly there would be a furious burst of activity. She would stride back and forth, climb ladders, spray, dribble, sweep, stroke, splash paint, and pencil in enormous lines, rub chalk, pastel, charcoal, bring forth figures amazing to the eye.

Then ...

Then she would stop, withdraw, frown, chew at her lip, grow moody, pout, go for long walks alone; refuse to talk; lock herself in the bathroom; or walk up and down kicking at pebbles. Until, suddenly, she would look up, grin, and say, "Hi!"

That's the way it was.

He glanced at his watch, faintly visible ...

Now it would be ... about dinnertime ...

She would be feeding the kids ...

Kids ... And married ... to a man she loved.

She had sent him a card with one of the little stick drawings she did so well. It showed a little stick man and a little stick woman climbing a ladder towards an immense and smiling sunflower that towered over them – in the eye of the flower was spelled out in vibrant colored capitals "Hi!"

"Hi! I'm back!"

"Hi!"

No doubt about it – as far as human beings went, she was one of the most beautiful of them all. He lit a new candle, placed it carefully in front of the photograph, and walked out to the terrace and sat down. Perhaps he was falling asleep. His chin slipped down on to his chest. He woke with a start and looked up at the stars.

The hours became unclear after that.

Much later he took the candle into the bathroom. The peeing took a long time and the stream of piss, bright yellow in the candlelight, looked rich and steamy. He flushed the toilet and looked at himself in the mirror.

The candlelight cast shadows that made his face look different. He saw things he would not otherwise have seen. A line deep like a scar ran diagonally down his forehead: the fault-lines of the skull showed through, carved in lines in the flesh. He traced it with his finger. Fine lines and blue shadows under his eyes. He stroked the crisp gray stubble of his beard. The beard was new; he'd let it grow only in the last two weeks; already it looked old.

When he went back out onto the terrace, he realized that his bones were aching and it was almost dawn. The air had a milky burnt coolness and the night animals had fallen silent and those of the day had not yet woken.

He pulled on a bathing suit and his shorts and put on the straw hat and got into the Volkswagen.

He drove along the empty cool roads to the beach and walked in through the empty restaurant where nobody seemed to be awake. He walked across the restaurant terrace and down to the sea, slipped out of the shorts and walked into the water and swam along until he saw the piece of white driftwood up near the dunes.

He came up out of the water dripping and slightly out of breath feeling as if he were much younger than he was and as if something significant might happen. He walked up to the driftwood and then continued to the dunes. He saw the cottage and that the windows were all shuttered and bolted and that the Land Rover was gone.

He crouched on the dune for a long time playing with handfuls of sand. The sun came up and its heat lay on his forehead. A stray dog, mangy and covered with bloated tics, stopped, considered him quizzically with its brown eyes, wagged its tail, and then wandered off, across the dunes, and out of sight.

Later he walked back to the restaurant and bought a bottle of chilled white wine from the barman and went down and sat on the beach in a deckchair facing the sea.

He was the only person on the beach.

It was the beginning of another day.

The barman was polishing glasses but he walked out – polishing a glass – and stood on the terrace and looked at the back of the head of the man who was sitting far down on the beach slouched in a deckchair staring at the sea. The man was holding the bottle by the neck, limply, the bottom of the bottle trailing on the sand.

The barman straightened a few chairs and went back inside to polish glasses. He stood at the bar and he polished glasses. He wondered if this man who came and didn't say anything and drank bottles of expensive chilled white wine all alone would become a regular customer.

Out on the beach, the man pulled down his straw hat. Nothing much happens when you watch the sun but it is interesting to watch all the same. Through the interstices of straw-strewn gold, the waves of the sea were small and broke the sun up into a thousand tiny sparkles, which filled his eyes. Warmed by the sun, the straw hat smelled like sunlight and like fields of straw and like a childhood that maybe once he had had, and maybe he hadn't. As he dozed, in the sparkling jewels of straw, the sun and the sea danced, mingled together, merged, and became one – yes, they became one, in the obliterating purity of light, they became – *eternity*.

SHATTERED

It Must Have Been the Rain

IT MUST HAVE BEEN THE RAIN.

I get my pills so I won't kill people. That's a joke. Ha, Ha, Ha. I don't think I killed any people, not before, not wanting to, no ... not wanting to. People die, they tell me, but not by me! Ha! Ha! Ha! Otherwise I wouldn't be out, would I?

'Cause I'm out now!

When I went out it was raining and I got on the bus. I stood by the sign and got on the bus. It wasn't a bus because it goes on tracks like a train but it goes on streets like a bus so it's like a bus; it's a ... it's a ... ?

It's a *streetcar*, now I remember. I like streetcars, I remember. I remember, too, sometimes, what I like and what I don't like. But not always. So I climbed up the streetcar steps and showed the card they gave me and I sat down. I looked out the window at the rain, the stoplights pulled up and changed from red to green and went by. I was all wet and could feel the water dripping off me.

"Stupid. You don't even have an umbrella."

"Mind your own business."

It was raining and I got on the bus, the streetcar. A woman sits down beside me. She has white hair soft like candy floss. A truck is outside the window it has a mouse on the side with big ears on it and it goes. The mouse looks at me. Then the mouse is gone. The woman with candy-floss hair looks at me out of the side of her eyes; she has a purse in her lap and she's holding on tight. I look at her and she looks away.

This is the street where the crazies go.

The loony bin is on this street.

All the crazies ride up and down.

It's raining.

I can see inside people's thoughts; not all the time, like the fat man on the other side of the streetcar; he has a newspaper and he's scratching the back of his neck where the hair's shaved and the rolls of fat are over his dirty striped white-and-blue collar and there's drops of rain stuck like drops of snot in his hair it's so greasy and black and thick, I don't know what he's thinking but sometimes I can see thoughts so clear it's painful and I don't want to think about it ever.

Outside the window it's raining.

The woman with the candy-floss hair looks at me, nods, and looks away. I'm next to the window so I look out. I can see my face, part of my face, in the window. And the rain.

It's raining.

I like rain.

The candy-floss woman's hands are sort of jumpy on her purse.

"You scare people."

"I do not!"

"You do. You're too big."

I look down at myself: I'm not too big. I feel my face crinkle up and I know I'm going to cry but I don't cry I just sniffle and wipe my nose. Snot. I look at the snot on my fingers. Snot is like glass – you can see through it.

"Sissy!" she says.

She is just about the ugliest thing I ever saw in my life.

"I am not. I am not," I say.

"Sissy!" she says

She's real small and she likes to make me cry; I think she wants me to hit her.

"Stupid!" she says. Her legs are real skinny and her knees look like two knots. She has two front teeth hang over her lip that she gives me and I'd like to knock out. I close my fists into two big tight heavy balled fists like somebody called them once. "Two big balled fists," he said.

"Stupid," she says, "You are real stupid."

I don't say anything, just look at her and those big baggy shorts she wears, man's hand-me-downs too big for a little person like her.

"I wasn't so stupid before," I say.

"Before!" She snorts a noise like she was gonna eat up a rope of her own snot. Snot is pretty. It can be green too or white like sugar. "Before!" She makes a face. "There is no before. Before is a long way away from where you are now. Where you are now, is crazy, you stupid you!"

She talks at me in my head even when she's not here; one reason I don't kill her is if she died she'd still be talking at me in my head. Guy said a joke about death and taxes or something in front of the television and I thought that one thing's sure too is her talking, she talks like she'll never stop, not even dead she won't stop, not in my head, I can hear her all the time, and I can see her too, in my head, not even closing my eyes do I need to do to see her, I see her with my eyes wide open, in front of other things that are really here like she was a transparent glass person, anytime, I can see the way she scratches herself behind one knee or rubs her knuckle across her wet nose and wiggles it. I can think things I can't say and see things too, so many things, after that accident they say was the thing that did it.

"How old are you?" I say.

"Eighteen." Her two front teeth stare at me.

"You look like shit," I say.

She looks at me and then she walks away and I didn't see her for three days I think and I thought I did a bad thing and now I know. Now I know.

"You look like shit." Next time I said.

"You too," she said; those funny teeth I think were smiling, the lip drawn up, like the better to bite me with. Then she got serious. "It's not true you look like shit. You're very, very beautiful you know," she said, "You are the most beautiful thing in the world. In the whole wide world."

"Not true," I said; she was leading up to something so she could laugh at me, I know that. Say little nice things then one big bad thing. I understand some things real good but I know lots of things I don't understand. I was mad she didn't run away when I said you look like shit. "You look like shit," I said again, but she stood there.

"It's true," she said; she turned her back on me. Her elbows are like lemon-pips. "You're beautiful but people can see you're crazy," she said from behind her back. So that was what she was going to say; I knew it, and I looked at the back of her neck where the hair curls down and she turned around but she was not laughing she was just looking at me with those big eyes – they were sort of sad.

"You look like shit," I said.

"Yeah, I sure do. I sure do look like shit." Her eyes were wet but she didn't run away.

I went and looked in the mirror in the bathroom four doors down from my room to see if I could see the crazy in my face. I couldn't see any crazy, just the scar which starts where the hair starts and you can only see a bit of that.

Maybe I should have a sign around my neck saying "CRAZY." I don't care about the scar anymore. Once she touched it and I

said don't touch that and I hit her not hard but I hit her and I was
sorry after but she didn't tell anybody or even cry, just looked at
me like I was something really sad that she was seeing for the first
time. The scar looks funny like it was painted on. So bright!

Ha, ha, ha, I'm laughing until somebody flushes the toilets and
I know somebody is there so I go back out into the corridor and
think maybe I will go outside but no it is already night and the
door is locked.

The stoplights change in the rain and we go on. People have rain-
coats and umbrellas over them. They duck their heads down. The
lady with the purse has stopped looking at me; she has rings on her
fingers and her purse has a gold clip; there is fat puffed up around
the rings and I wonder if she ever takes them off or if you'd have to
cut the finger off to get the ring.

"I like the rain," I say. The rain is silver gray. "If the rain's real
warm you can go out without any clothes on. You ever done that?"

The lady with the white hair like candy floss doesn't look at me
but her face goes stiff and she gets up and goes to another seat. I
guess I'm being crazy again. Crazy is maybe like a traffic light it
goes off and on, on and off, off and on. Sometimes I think I understand things and then I know I don't, which I guess is part of being
crazy. I didn't understand the lady with the white candy-floss hair
was with two little girls – must be about eight or nine – they have
hair – blond like hers is white – except theirs is straight down to
their shoulders where hers is all up on top of her head in curls. They
look like blond girls in pictures. She sits close to them and they look
at her and she says something and they look at me and look away.

Little girls, I like little girls.

But little girls make me sad. Blond little girls make me real sad.

It rains again and they are gone and the lady with the white hair
like candy floss who saw the craziness in my face. We go fast through
a green light that's just turned green. People run. The rain is close

against the window. I put my hand on the cool of the window. Windows keep the rain out but you can see things even through the rain.

I like to ride on the streetcar in the rain or sunshine and I don't want to get off.

We go up over a bridge and down.

The bells clang and there are sparks. People get on and get off and look at me out of the corner of their eyes and nobody sits next to me.

The streetcar is empty and it swings into a yard with big red brick walls and the big walls come out toward the streetcar and there are lots of other streetcars in the yard on tracks under the rain not going anywhere.

The driver tells me it's the end of the line. Nobody else is in the streetcar. I stand up and get off and I don't know where I am. The driver is standing scratching his head and looking at me and I walk past the big high brick walls out onto the street and the lights are on in the streetcar when I look back and it looks like a home you could go into and sleep; then I'm farther on and it's just big walls and the streetcar is gone. The rain is warm. I look up at the sky. I want to take off my clothes but that would be crazy because I know what crazy is. Not all the time I think but now I do. People can see the crazy in me anyway so it doesn't matter what I do but I like the rain so I don't want people to come and take me away. So I don't take my clothes off. *"That is being real smart,"* she says, *"thinking about things before they happen."* Sometimes I get my shit together like she says I get it together and I think about things and they happen or don't happen because I think about them. Otherwise things just come at you and it's too late.

Big signs on walls and the rain coming down the walls like waves of silver ; the rain is so fast I can hardly see. On the face of the girl on the wall they painted black eyes black nose black teeth like the guy was killing the painted girl in the jeans, he painted her out, she's like a skull, her fingers are still hooked in the rim of the jeans but you can't see what she looks like anymore because the guy has painted her nose mouth eyes, painted her dead. They painted her dead with a spray gun painted dead all those teeth she had. Like a skull. You know it's not real dead anyway just painted dead like you can draw on a piece of paper. Real dead makes me real sad. I walk away from the tracks and the lights and down a smaller, quieter, darker street.

It's a real small street and narrow and I don't like it, but I'm in here now and I don't like turning around and going back the way I came.

Some guys are under an awning.

It's a beer place or liquor.

They laugh so I move away.

"Hey, big boy, come on over here."

I move away and I'm down at the end of the street which doesn't go anywhere. There's a big wall with a bottle of beer and a smile on it but you can't see the eyes, they faded away sometime long ago, the eyes.

"Hey, big boy!"

I turn and turn away; there's just the wall; I turn back and he's coming at me, one of them, walking through the rain, his fists bunched into balls, he has big broken teeth with holes between them; the other ones are laughing. He has white string for a belt tied loose and floppy and jeans and on his arm a tattoo looks like he made it himself.

I turn away, but he's got me by the shoulder and he's ripping my shirt.

The rain is warm but I don't want my shirt ripped. "Go away," I say. I think about the streetcar and how warm it looked and about my room and how gray it is but warm and dry and not in the rain. In my room with the light off I can look out at the rain and at the trees. I think about her. *"Beautiful,"* she says in my head, *"You're real beautiful."* I get mad and I think he shouldn't rip my shirt, it's not right.

He is laughing. *"Go away,* he says! Ha, ha, ha. Big stupid idiot!" He is still pulling on my shirt.

"Stupid," she says in my head, *"You're real stupid."*

She has that grin on her lips I wanna punch those two stupid teeth but not really, not really ...

I hit him over the head, then across the side of the head. His eyes are round and there's blood and he falls down in the rain on his face. It's asphalt, black asphalt, like fresh tar. I smell the tar from days when they must have laid it down. In sunshine probably. Guys with no shirts in sunshine hot on bare skin and the nice hot smell of tar.

I start to run but they grab at me and catch my clothes and they knock me down and start kicking and I kick back and then I curl up and there's nothing and time stops. Just stars like I was floating in some great painful place I remember from before. *"Stupid,"* she says. *"Where are you now, stupid?"*

∞

Where are you?

So this is night. So this is night and rain in my face. The night tastes of blood running in my face and I am looking up into the night and maybe I'm blind because all I see is night and rain. But no, rain is not blindness. I feel pain too, pain in my chest, pain in my arms. I cough and I feel I'm coughing blood. Shit, I get up, up on my hands and knees. Nothing but rain, shit. What the fuck happened? Then I remember I'm dead already and crazy. I get up on my hands and knees and I'm in some sort of dead-end street. I sit and I crawl, and I get up and I sit against a wall, close to some garbage cans. My head is totally clear as if there was nothing in it. I've not got any clothes on at all, or almost no clothes, just underpants, soiled stained underpants. Must have shit myself, or is that blood? Too big for me too. Doesn't smell of shit. So what am I doing here? It's warm rain. Warm rain. What the fuck does that remind me of? I try to stand up but it's too much. My head hurts.

I sit against the wall.

The rain comes down.

Maybe somebody will come. Maybe somebody will tell me and I'll remember.

This is a brain shift, a shifting in my head, but it won't last, it won't last.

Some things I should remember. Like who I am and how I got here wherever here is. Jesus, my head feels clear, but bad, bad, bad. This must be one hell of a hangover, how could I feel so bad and not know who I am?

A headlight glares and I raise my arm and it hurts but I raise it and like a blinding flash sort of I see, I see with great clarity, the headlight, then, I see the little girl's face, in a car, in the front seat, strapped in. The car is swerving, into headlights, into oncoming headlights, the little girl's eyes are wide and what is that? – It's terror, pure terror, that's what it is.

I am driving that car.

Is it me?

The car is skidding, skidding, icy pavement, black like a dark sea. Skidding, skidding, skidding.

"Daddy!"

WHAM! The light crinkles into a millions sparklers.

I killed her.

Didn't mean to of course. After all, she was my daughter and I loved her. It was our night out together, once a week I had the right, I had the duty, to take her out, and to get her back, by ... back by ...

Eight o'clock.

December, early December.

A slippery, slick street. I'd had a bit to drink, yes, not too much, just a bit, and I was late, so I was hurrying, hurrying to get there, mad too, I was mad at the bitch, on the phone, complaining, and ...

"Jack, you promised!"

A name ... Jack?

"Jack, you've been drinking! You shit!"

A name ...

"You absolute shit!"

A name?

"Jack, how could you do that? Drinking! You absolute shit!" Telephone voice, the bitch.

We went to a party. I took her to a party. She didn't want to come with me, but she came, she had to, she was only eight years old, couldn't refuse, could she, so she came to the party, and there were kids, and after a while she played with them and I flirted with that ... with some woman and had a drink or two and my woman, my ex-woman, ex-wife, ex-friend, she said she could smell the liquor over the phone, she could smell it, she said. I clutched the phone, hard, like I was going to break it: Fuck her!! I hung up.

The little girl was frightened when we got in the car. It's raining, icy rain. Shouldn't be frightened of daddy, honey, not of daddy, but I was mad as hell at her, fucking stupid cunt, fucking stupid cow ... at ...

Already dark. Comes in so early. It's raining, winter rain.

Car accelerates nicely.

You feel like a god.

Speed is like a god. Good acceleration.

Mercedes S Class, best money can buy!

Fuck!

Hate that bitch! Fuck her, fuck, fuck ...

Rev it, race it, rough it ...

God this is good!

Daddy!

What?

Don't go so fast – please!

That's okay, darling, we're okay, we're cool.

Slippery slick street glossy dark as a seal's pelt, street lamps wrought-iron old-fashioned circles of white light on asphalt, all gentrified, really classy, this neighborhood, slight downhill slope, not graded as well as it should be, these tires are new, the brakes ...

Slipping, skidding ... can't be ...

It all happened in slow-motion and there's nothing you can do. It must have been the rain.

Out of control. Jumped the guard-rail, into the opposite lane, and ...

"Daddy!" Screaming now. Car swirling around.

Big tractor-trailer, heavy bugger, way up, just the headlights, somehow I see the guy's face, pale terrified oval, mouth open, swinging the wheel. No way.

"Daddy!" Screaming now.

WHAM! A million sparklers.

It's not Christmas decorations. No.

And nothing.

The skid – it must have been the rain.

And you wake up you are somebody else. In fact, you never really woke up at all, I guess, because it was not you who woke up. *"You are real stupid, you know,"* a voice says, a girl's voice.

I start to cry.

My brain must be wrong. I sit against the wall crying and I don't even fucking know my own name – "Jack" – must be "Jack." And I don't know if I'm making up that stuff about the little girl and the accident or ... a wife, a divorce, a daughter, an accident, I was mad, I drank, I frightened her, then ...

And then ...

It must have been the rain.

∞

"*Real stupid.*"

Whose fucking voice is that? Sounds like a young boy or a woman, a very young woman. Voices in my head is all I need. Do I know you?

"*Yeah. You know me. Buck teeth, remember.*"

"Buck teeth?"

"*Two buck teeth with a gap between. You said I looked like shit.*"

"You probably do look like shit. Whoever you are."

"*I do, I do. I do look like shit. But you love me. Only you don't know it yet.*"

I lean against the wall. The rain comes down. Somebody from another fucking life; some crazy cunt of a voice; I must be crazy.

"*See, you're too stupid to know anything. You're an angel. That's what angels are. Stupid. Stupid, and innocent.*"

"Fuck you!"

"*I'm in love with an angel!*" The voice says it like it was a gay little kids' song. "*I'm in love with an angel!*" Sing-song, like a child, sing-song, like a child teasing a child.

"Fuck you!" I say, "Fuck off!"

I try to stand up but I sit down again and my eyes fill with blood. I think it's blood I don't know maybe pressure or something broke in my head anyway there are stars too, though not in the sky, it's raining. Raining, I like the warm rain, Maybe I can get back where I was maybe though now it's late and the doors will be locked and they punish you for that. What am I thinking? What?

Think things in your head. Otherwise they come at you too fast.

She said something like that – whoever she is and I don't know. I don't know anything only this circle of light and the rain falling. Slowly I get up without even thinking and I start to walk. I'll just walk. One leg hurts. I walk. Limping, I walk and I walk and I get lost somewhere down by the bridge so I lie down.

The rain is falling beyond the bridge but here under the bridge it is dry and smells like concrete dust and moist wood and old piss. And the river is like mud and moves slowly, mud-brown light, swirling, reflecting ...

∞

Sun ... the sun ...

The sun comes under the bridge and the sun is warm and I get up I'm not in my room, where am I, there's the river so I'm not far, and here it smells like grass and I like grass and sun. I walk to the water and the sun is on the water in ripples and I should go back but I feel sad like I lost something but I don't remember what I lost or if it was anything at all. I don't have a shirt or pants or jacket or shoes or socks so I don't have my card so how'll I get on the bus no, it's not a bus it's a ... it's on the street on tracks so it's ... yes, yes, it's a *street-car*, it's a streetcar, maybe if the driver knows me he'll let me on. I climb back up to the street from the river and stand on the side of the road. A streetcar comes and the driver looks at me when I get on but he doesn't say anything. I think I know him from somewhere and he looks at me in the mirror and I sit down next to the window and look out at the sunshine. Store fronts go by. It's hot against the window. People wear short-sleeves and girls have long legs.

This is the street where the crazies live.

All the crazies walk up and down.

Up and down.

All the crazies.

"They can see the craziness in you," she says.

I see myself in the window next to my head that rattles and we go along and the stores pass us and the lights and we go through a stop-light flickering green. The sun hurts my eyes and I put up my hand.

A little girl is sitting not far from me she's holding a woman's hand probably her mother and she has blond hair and I think of something I can't remember like a taste of metal in my mouth, memories like that you can't get at are like tastes on the tongue or smells in the air and I look away out the window and I know my eyes are wet, but I don't touch them and water goes down my cheeks which is part of being crazy I guess.

∞

"What happened to you, stupid?" Two buck teeth with the hole between looks like a chipmunk or a cartoon. "So what happened to you?"

"I went away" I say but I don't know what I mean, saying it. What do I mean?

"Shit! You didn't go away."

"No?"

"No." She has her hands at her waist like two fists, two small white scrunched up fists.

"I remembered but I don't remember what I remembered but I remembered something."

"No," she says. Her eyes look shiny. "You didn't remember any-thing. You didn't remember anything at all." She looks serious now, not mad, she reaches out, touches my scar and it feels nice and cool the end of her fingers on my scar I should hit her for touching my scar like that but I don't. "You ain't got anything to remember, stu-pid." It's a smile on her face. She's smiling one of those sad smiles she has.

"No. I guess not."

"You ain't got nothing to remember."

"No."

"And you look like shit," she grins.

"Yeah, I look like shit."

I take my pills so I won't kill people. That's a joke, ha, ha, ha. I don't think I killed any people, not before, not wanting to, no, not wanting to. People die, they tell me, but not by me! Ha! Ha! Ha! Otherwise I wouldn't be out, would I?

'Cause I'm out now.

∞

The water.

We sit down and look at the water. She holds my hand and then takes her hand away and lays it on the café table flat next to the coffee mug and I see all the fingers spread out very white and thin like a child's fingers and I like to look at them.

"I look like shit too," she says. Her smile shows her teeth; her teeth are nice.

There are boats on the water. She turns her face and looks at the water and closes her eyes because the sun is on the water and then she turns and her eyes look at me and she smiles. Now I know but I don't know why I know when her smile is a real smile and this is a real smile. Her knees are close to mine under the table and we knock our knees together and it's a nice game and I don't ever want to get lost again.

"You got nothing to remember," she says.

"No," I say. The light of the sun is on my face. I turn my face to the sun and close my eyes. "No. I got nothing to remember. It must have been the rain."

A Universe of Smiles

STEIN WENT OUT TO MEET THEM AT THE AIRPORT. This was unusual, but, then, Curtis was a celebrity. And – you had to admit it – the guy had a real, if limited, talent.

Sitting in the back of the limousine, Stein closed his eyes. He could imagine a scene, any scene, and see exactly how Curtis would shoot it.

The heroine comes through the door in her frilly 1950's party dress, reacts; and, starting from an extreme close-up, the camera slowly dollies back to reveal ... the horror ... the horror!

Yeah, a guy like that was a priceless talent, a producer's dream. You always knew precisely what he would do, and exactly how he would do it.

Stein personally took Mr. and Mrs. Curtis and their eleven-year-old son, Jerry, to see the rented villa.

Curtis himself went out into the garden and walked around. Then he collapsed on a bench under an oleander and stared up at the pure blue sky.

Jerry followed Stein everywhere as if he expected an answer to some unasked question.

Mrs. Curtis complained about the color scheme. With her long, tanned, tapered fingers – carefully lacquered and with pointed nails – she touched all the walls.

From the terrace, Jerry looked longingly down at the wooded cliffs and gullies below. It looked like Robinson Crusoe country.

"A man could run away down there, and disappear. Forever." Stein crinkled his eyes and gave Jerry his I-understand-how-you'd-like-to-escape-from-that-bitch-of-a-mother smile.

Jerry grinned uncertainly and turned away. He stared with what seemed a tinge of guilt down towards the gullies.

Beyond the deep green tangle of wood and the brown earthy gashes, a bluish mist that claimed to be the Pacific Ocean merged into a bluish mist that claimed to be the Californian sky.

This is paradise, thought Stein. This is where the world ends.

He walked back inside where Mrs. Curtis was standing with her hands on her hips looking at the living room. "Mustard is not one of my favorite colors," said Mrs. Curtis.

Stein grinned a flat uncomprehending who-gives-a-fuck-about-color-schemes grin; although, if you cared to be charitable or naive, it could have been interpreted as a hopeless male-unable-to-under-stand-female-sensibilities grin, which was, he supposed, better, at least from a diplomatic point of view. He was tempted to add, as a flourish, an Italian-style – Neapolitan, really, he figured – shrug (shoulders hunched up, elbows squished to the sides, palms flat and slanted outward) signifying skepticism, indifference (who-gives-a-fuck), and abashed male hopelessness. But he didn't. She didn't deserve the effort, and she might take it the wrong way, which would be the right way, but that was not a way he wanted to go, not now.

"I'll send you some decorators," Stein said. He smiled his enough-of-all-this-let's-go-to-lunch smile.

∞

Sabatini's was unique in that it had a section for children.

As he was unfolding his napkin, Stein noticed there was only one child in the children's section. She was beautiful, and she was alone.

Though Stein could only see her profile, he could see in his mind's eye her big serious blue eyes, her oval face, her strong dark eyebrows, the honey-gold skin of her forehead and the way her long, straight flaxen hair was combed back. She looked like a Swedish or German princess, something pure and precious, something utterly beautiful and out of an ancient fairy tale.

She was twelve years old.

She had been totally deaf from birth, stone-deaf. She was a deaf-mute. Thinking about it, Stein smiled an I'm-considering-the-menu smile. But he did glance, once or twice, over the top of his gold-rimmed glasses, at the girl.

As she ate, she stared into the distance. The distance, in this case, was not very far away: it consisted of a stone wall, a carefully cultivated and over-bright tangle of climbing ivy, and a set of crossed Mexican swords.

Stein wondered what the girl was thinking.

He knew almost everything there was to know about her, everything he could find out anyway, because ...

... Stein noticed that Jerry was staring at the girl too. In the boy's eyes there was the same vague longing he'd had when he'd been looking at the gullies and the ghostly shadow and infinite promise of the Pacific.

Curtis was explaining how he was planning to shoot the rape scene. The young heroine – still a virgin – was running, stumbling, falling, then getting up again. She was running through a forest in the late fall. The only sound would be the crackling and rustling of the thick carpet of dry autumn leaves as the girl ran, stumbled, got up, stumbled again, got up. No sound except the leaves, and, perhaps, her breathing.

Behind her, the stranger would be gaining ground, coming closer, silently, inexorably, like the deadly hunter he was.

Ultra-smooth reverse tracking shot, Curtis was saying, skimming along at ground level, hugging the girl, strengthening the viewer's identification with her.

The low, gliding shot would not include the hunter, so the viewer would share the girl's uncertainty as to how close he was, as to what he was. There'd be no music, said Curtis. There would be just the pure horror of the long-drawn-out silent chase. There would be just the purity of the emotion, he was saying, just the purity of the emotion.

Yes, thought Stein, that's exactly the way Curtis would do it. It was a homage to Ingmar Bergman, acknowledged or unacknowledged. Borrow or steal, that's the key to genius.

The man had a Dewey Decimal System of images in his head. Stein tried to see it. He wondered if the sequence could work in color with the intensity it had in Bergman's black-and-white. Bergman had done it in black-and-white, hadn't he? Wouldn't all those bright crisp autumn leaves be too pretty, too garish? Wouldn't they distract from the effect? Like Hitchcock's *The Trouble with Harry*, it might be too garish to work. Maybe, Stein thought, it could be dusk, or misty. Maybe you could shoot in a cold bluish light. That way you could bring down the brightness of the colors, approximate the cold, forbidding, textured sculpture of black-and-white. Somewhere behind his eyeball, Stein replayed the Bergman sequence in his head. He wondered if he should suggest changes now or later. Sometimes the exercise of genius and power required tact.

"Mom?" Jerry shifted on his seat. "Can I go and eat over there?"

Mrs. Curtis glanced and saw the blond girl eating alone in the children's section. Stein held his breath and ran his tongue over his lips.

"No," said Mrs. Curtis, "You stay with us."

"But mom, it's for kids. That girl's all alone. She looks really nice. And I'm bored here listening to Dad and Mr. Stein."

"Listen to your mother," said Curtis wearily.

"Let him go and sit over there if he wants to," said Stein. He paused. He looked at Curtis. "Or else I fire you." He smiled his even-lipped you-don't-know-if-I-mean-it smile and let the smile freeze – it barely showed two rows of bright, perfect teeth – while he continued to stare amiably – crinkling his eyes ever so slightly – at Curtis.

Curtis looked at Stein for an instant. His pale blue eyes coming back from whatever cinematographic forest they had been traveling through. He cleared his throat. Mrs. Curtis made a convulsive movement with her serviette, and bit her lower lip.

Curtis glanced quickly at his wife, then back at Stein. "Sure, Jerry, you go over there. You're probably bored listening to me and Mr. Stein."

Jerry, humiliated for everybody (Himself, Mom, Dad, and Mr. Stein), looked at each of them in turn. Stein, enjoying the cruelty, turned the knife. He smiled his shucks-it-weren't-nothin smile at Jerry, glanced at Mrs. Curtis, and said, with his wistful, dreamy I-wish-we'd-known-each-other-way-back-when smile, "You know, I was young too once ..."

The tension in Mrs. Curtis dissolved. She smiled back. Sometimes, thought Stein, it was like being God. Stein the charmer. Never known to fail ...

Almost never.

∞

As he continued listening to Curtis, Stein kept his eye on Jerry. Balancing his plate carefully, the kid walked up to the table and said something to the girl.

Until the last second, she didn't see him coming. She was lost in her dream-world or thought-world, or whatever it was.

She jumped slightly, and blinked in a frightened way. But she was quick. She recovered herself, smiled, and gestured at Jerry to sit down.

Jerry was clearly puzzled by the lack of words, but he sat down, put his own plate in the place across from hers, and smiled.

She handed him one of the little cards that explained that she couldn't hear and couldn't speak. Jerry read it. His eyes went round. Maybe he was frightened: how should he behave? The girl used her smile, which was brilliant, thought Stein, an A-1 smile if ever there was one, and Jerry visibly relaxed. He then obviously asked her if she could understand him. Yes, she could, she nodded. She wrote it down: "I can read lips."

Then, undoubtedly, she had explained about sign language. Stein could imagine their dialogue, just as he had imagined it – and dialogues like it – a thousand times.

He and Curtis went over the budget. They discussed possible musical scores. They discussed details of how the heroine should dress.

Mrs. Curtis listened idly. From time to time she cast a nervous glance towards her son. He seemed to be learning some strange new game with his hands. They were fluttering around in the air in front of his face. The girl smiled, wrote things down, and fluttered back.

Stein glanced at Mrs. Curtis. She was in fact a very pretty woman. Perhaps she had been made bitter by being closed out of the inner world of a dreamer like Curtis. Stein remembered she had briefly been a successful model, and then a junior editor at Random House. Then she had married Curtis. Finis! The End! Kaput!

Stein flashed her a quick I-see-how-beautiful-you-are smile – sideways tilt of the head, half-closing of the eyes, almost boyishly shy grin – and said, "You know, Joan, I've been thinking (thoughtful pause), we need some readers, people who can spot and suggest a good story, do a preliminary analysis, you know. Would you be interested?"

She was startled. It had come out of the blue. Curtis was imme-diately enthusiastic. He always been telling her, he said, that she needed to start working again. As he listened to Curtis wax enthu-siastic about his wife's talent, Stein thought he might just learn to like the guy.

The conversation continued on this reassuring subject for a while. Then Mrs. Curtis – now rebaptized "Joan" – asked, "Is the girl a deaf-mute?"

"Yes," said Stein. "She's Michelle's daughter," he added, nod-ding towards a very famous and very beautiful actress sitting with her equally famous husband in a niche six tables away.

"Do you think it's risky for Jerry?" She asked, glancing at the girl. "I mean, a deaf-mute ... And the girl is very beautiful."

"Well, they're just kids." Stein smiled a gentle, almost pater-nal smile. Jerry, he knew, was a very expensive kid, sent to the best schools, with special tutors, to force him into becoming a six-or-sev-en-figure-income Midtown Manhattan genius, a Master of the Uni-verse. "And the little girl, well, I understand she has a stratospheric IQ."

Joan was pacified. Jerry was known, among their friends in New York, as somewhat of a prodigal, and meeting a deaf-mute girl – the daughter of Michelle Lombard – would undoubtedly broaden his horizons. Joan – Stein could see her mind working – had undoubt-edly read somewhere – oh, yes, in that book by Oliver Sacks, that the deaf-mute language was rich in semantic and perceptual nuances that even the most sophisticated spoken languages ...

Stein smiled his I-understand-the-fears-the-hopes-of-a-protec-tive-mother smile. He put his hand lightly on Joan's.

∞

As they were about to leave, Jerry went through a long ceremony of adieux with his new friend. When he came up to them, it was clear he was in love, the way you can be in love when you are eleven years old. Stein envied the kid: what a sense of awe and mystery and wonder there can be when you are eleven years old. It was what Stein called the Robinson Crusoe effect, you were suddenly cast away alone in the world and that world was bright and shiny and new. It was infinite. The beach and sky stretched away forever. And what could be more infinite than a beautiful young woman who couldn't speak?

Yeah, I'm jealous, thought Stein, smiling a crisp, happy smile at Jerry.

∞

It was a dark night, humid, and clinging, when Stein returned to his big, empty villa, forty miles away, perched alone on cliffs overlooking the Pacific.

He stripped and changed into an old pair of plaid bathing trunks. He walked out onto the terrace, stood at the parapet, and looked out where, beyond the trees, the ocean hung invisible, a palpable manifestation of darkness.

Stein swam seven lengths of the pool. Then he sat on the edge of the pool for a long time. He let his legs dangle in the water. Finally, he made himself a very dry martini. He smiled his now-I'm-alone-with-my-own-thoughts smile. Wistful, maybe.

Funny, he thought, how you could understand everybody else, orchestrate and control their feelings, but not your own. Everything outside him was limpid and clear. He knew exactly how images and sounds would work on a matron in Manhattan, on a young couple in Des Moines, on an angry black kid in Harlem, on a left-wing intellectual on the Left Bank in Paris ... He knew what a slow dolly backwards could do, what a shot tracking backwards while zooming in could do, what a close-up angled upwards ... He knew exactly how his smiles – his repertoire of smiles – would work upon anyone, how each smile could frighten them, seduce them, reassure them, cow them. He wondered if a catalogue of smiles existed, a universal catalogue of smiles.

He stroked his jaw. His face felt tired from all those smiles. He stood up, went to the bar, and made himself another dry martini. This one was even drier than the first.

As he put in the olive he realized that he was now thinking of smiles as a cartoonist might think of them. There was a Mickey Mouse smile, a Dagwood and Blondie smile, a Doonesbury smile, a Dick Tracy smile. Betty Boop had a smile, and Woody Woodpecker. Snoopy had a smile. Did Pig-Pen have a smile? A sort of crinkled little stroke of the pen? You could line all the smiles up and look at them, and put a label under each one. He wondered if – behind their smiles – cartoon characters had souls. That was a tricky theological question. Yes, he decided after some reflection, they must have souls, cartoon souls. Gentle little precipitates, or abstracts, or excerpts, from the secret souls of their makers. Something like that. Carefully he sipped at the edge of the martini.

Watching rushes in his private screening room, it often occurred to Stein that beautiful women had smiles like clowns. Exaggerated, gorgeous, unforgettable.

Or was it that clowns had smiles like women? He'd read somewhere that clowns were androgynous. Symbolically speaking, of course. He wondered if there was an evolutionary reason for the big beautiful female smile. There must be. Did smiles – in all their infinite variety – serve the survival of the species or its DNA or some particular gene or whatever it was that was hell-bent on surviving?

Outside, on other peoples' faces, it seemed to Stein that everything had a cartoon-like clarity. It was as if he could read their minds.

With his own face too, he knew what he was doing. But, now, at this moment, if he looked inward, there was nothing. Nothing inside him but a thick mist, an invisible pressure, like the vast Pacific hanging there, unseen, dark and close, in the humid night.

The self, like the ocean, was somewhere just beyond the reach of his senses.

He walked to the parapet and stared out into the darkness. If he listened closely enough, he imagined he might even hear the waves. Impossible of course.

Only once, thirteen years before, during his brief and secret and torrid affair with Michelle had he known inner clarity. But even that was an illusion. He had known neither clarity nor peace nor freedom.

Maybe it was a trade-off, he thought. Maybe if you had a talent like his – and Stein had a talent, a multi-million dollar talent – maybe, if you had a talent like that, it had to be based on some inner loss, some inner corruption, some ... some inner absence.

He had loved Michelle. Like he'd loved nobody before. Like nobody since.

No, not true. Now he did love somebody, somebody he would never know; somebody he could only love from a distance ... An imaginary love ...

A fairy-tale love – deep in the forests of the night ...

It was a love sublimated and sublime, innocent and unrealized, suggestive as a poem or a pencil sketch by a genius, just a line here, a line there, the rest forever incomplete, fragments to dream on ...

Like a cartoon.

Like the horizon.

Like infinity ...

With Michelle it ended badly.

One smoky autumn night – he was barbecuing a steak on the

terrace – the first star had just appeared in the West – Michelle came up to him, put her hands on his shoulders, and told him she was pregnant. She was blushing, grinning a mischievous grin, and, before he could react, she hugged him. She wanted to goof around, play the clown, celebrate, be celebrated, and be comforted.

He pushed her away. He was horrified. He threw a tantrum. He didn't want the child! She was married. She had her career to think of! What would her husband say, or do! It would be a goddamn scandal. Her husband was powerful, goddamn it! Stein threatened to end the relationship. Michelle begged him, she got down on her knees, she got down on her fucking knees. She was so beautiful, down on her knees, begging, tearful, it was painful to look at. He told her he didn't love her. *Why? Why?* He still didn't know. It was a lie of course. Why had he done it? *Why?*

That night Michelle took an overdose, a very serious overdose ... She would have died. But her husband's night flight to New York was canceled due to fog. He came home, and ... he found her.

She came out of it, fit as a fiddle, with a new, strange haunted look. And she hated Stein. Hers was the sort of passionate love that – when it is betrayed – turns into ferocious hate and never forgives. Her eyes had a depth now they had never had before, her expressions and gestures had a gravity, even a humor and irony, unmatched by any actress her age. Her career, from that day on, was pure gold.

But the baby ...

It was a girl ...

Upon the foetus, such chemicals, the doctors said, have the effect of ... and ... but it's only a hypothesis ... and ...

Somewhere it says that the sins of the fathers ...

To have all that beauty, and ...

What was it like, Stein wondered, never to hear anything? Never to have heard anything? Not a word, not a note, not the twittering of a bird, not the wind in the grass, not the waves on a beach, not the voice of someone you loved ...

Stein plunged into the pool. He swam five more lengths, under-water. He skimmed the bottom. He kept as deep as he could. He held his breath.

Michelle's husband insisted on assuming the girl's paternity. Now she was his daughter. She was their only child. He agreed too with Michelle that Stein was never again to appear in their lives. Never.

It was the one time Stein did not smile. But he acquiesced. What else could he do? And he put his best face on it.

Stein climbed out of the pool. He toweled himself roughly with a heavy coarse towel. Thoughtfully, he walked to the end of the terrace.

Leaning against the parapet, he strained his eyes to see if he could catch a single hint of the ocean, a light, a glimmer, the weight of a shadowy horizon, the silhouette of a rocky promontory. But he could see nothing, nothing at all.

Well, it was a dark night. Stein swallowed the last of his martini. He rinsed the glass carefully. He turned out the lights. He stood for a moment on the terrace. Then he turned his back to the night, and, smiling a peculiar smile, a very special, haunted smile, Stein walked to his bed alone.

What Time is it On the Moon?

THE MAN LOOKS UP AT THE MOON. By all rights the moon shouldn't be there; the moon is trespassing on the day – dusk, really, the ending of the day, and the beginning of dusk. It's a half moon too, which compounds the crime, the impropriety.

"Dad, what time is it on the moon?"

The man looks up at the moon and then at the street. When the sun is down at the west end of Queen Street you can tell which way the world is tilted by the way the sun sets. You can tell the season by the way the sun glints on the streetcar tracks, the angle and the quality of the light, yellow and rose, green and blue, delicate or harsh. There might not be a snowflake, it might be warm, even balmy, and still you could tell it was winter.

"What time is it on the moon?"

The man thinks: The light counts, the way the light falls, the tones and the blendings. The man is drinking tea. Well, he's not yet drinking; he's waiting for the bag to stain the water. From time to time, he lifts the lid and looks in the little pot.

The little boy sitting in front of the man is sucking coke from a can through a bendable bright blue-and-white striped plastic straw.

It is twilight time, or almost. The man remembers an old song; it was a song when the man was a child; old songs like that particular song make the man twitchy and uncomfortable in his skin and in his ill-fitting clothes; twilight – even the idea of twilight – brings tears to his eyes; but the man never lets the tears show and he never cries; the man remembers from decades ago long drives in the family car – it was twilight time – his nose was pressed against the window of the car. The farm houses and fields and barns and small main street stores and circles of lamp-light moved past the car while his mother and father, seated stiffly in the front seats, say that they are having a very nice drive. "This is a very nice drive," says mother. "Yes, this is a very nice drive," says father.

"There's no time on the moon," says the man.

The boy's straw slurps and gurgles; the boy wipes at his nose.

"You want another coke?" says the man; he looks at his watch.

The boy shakes his head; the striped blue-and-white straw dangles from his lip; the boy takes it out of his mouth and looks at it.

The terrace umbrellas flutter in the warm breeze. The striped blue-and-white awnings move, ripping like waves on the sea; the light at the end of the street breaks into square chunks of pale gold, long ribbons of silky black, and yellow misty shades of green; the sky overhead is dark already and the street lights flicker on suddenly and seem too bright. The breeze is warm and it makes the man think of faraway places; it brings other twilight times to mind: people come, people go; everybody is heading somewhere; everybody has somebody somewhere; everybody has some place to go to, someone to meet; someone to love – or to hate. The moon is brighter now, braver, a haughty metal-white curlicue in the sky.

The boy in the past – the boy the man once was – with his nose pressed against the window of the car – watches the fields slip by, the wheat and hay waving gently, shimmering a deeper gold in the breeze, and the green grass catching the last light of day and thickening and brightening in color with the onrushing darkness and promise of impending night; beyond the fields are woods and forests, and in the forests are rivers and streams, rippling in the shadows and splashes of moonlight. The boy he was then wants to be far away; he wants to run naked through the woods; he wants to meet strange beautiful lustful unknown creatures though he does not know what the words mean, or even what the thoughts are; he wants adventure and he wants each day and night to be new and strange with an awesome, flesh-thrilling beauty and enticement. Behind the windows of the car, driving through the dusk, the boy is in prison. He is about to become a man and without knowing it he wants to break out of the cocoon that is childhood. Still trapped in a child's body and mind are intimations and fragments of manhood, a burgeoning future and a child's imagination, a clumsy awkward hopeless amalgam.

The boy pulls the blue-and-white plastic straw out of the tin can and puts it down on the folded white paper napkin and turns and looks at the moon; he looks at a clock on the top of a building; it is 9:00 o'clock; it is late; here on the street it is late. The face of the clock is round like a full moon, but tonight the moon is not full, not round. Sometimes the moon is round. Sometimes the moon isn't round. Sometimes the moon is half a moon; sometimes, it's a quarter moon, and sometimes there is no moon at all. The boy looks at the man; then he looks at the moon.

The man looks at his watch. The woman should already have come; she should be here soon; she can take the boy back. He has nothing to say to the boy; what can you say to a child? The man tries to remember the old days when he was a child, but those days are long ago and that boy who lived so long ago is a stranger to him now; that boy is dead, that boy with his nose pushed against the glass, that boy who dreamed of fields, woods, satyrs, nymphs, adventures, narrow escapes, cliff-hanging episodes, scantily clad demoiselles, ruined castles and endless underground caverns, and of worlds to explore, beyond the stars. "We had a very nice drive." He remembers the phrase with a shiver and looks at the boy; the boy is pretending to look at the moon. "We are having a very nice drive," says mother. "Yes, we are having a very nice drive," says father.

The woman comes. The man is surprised at how his pulse still quickens, at how he gets a lump in his throat, when he sees her, when he hears her voice.

The boy is running towards the woman; he jumps up as she bends down to kiss him; she kneels, wraps her arms around him.

They laugh; the boy is telling her something; she laughs again, casts a reproving, smiling glance at the man.

The sun has disappeared now; even the rosy reflections high on the buildings are gone. The sky has turned the deep blue and indigo of early evening, the neon is bright and the trees make sharp shadows – blinking neon and serrated sidewalk shadows.

The woman and the boy come to the man's table. "So you took him up on the Ferris wheel?" she says, falsely scolding, standing close.

The man is always embarrassed when he sees her; he is embarrassed by her beauty, by her laughter which is so rich, so free, by the things she says which seem always to have so many hidden teasing and unspoken meanings. She is inside his head, inside his skin still, even now.

He half stands up, kisses her on the cheek; she smiles, kisses him back, and lightly puts her warm dry palm to the side of his face.

Yes, he took the boy up the Ferris wheel.

∞

Alone, he finishes his tea. Then he sits for a long time watching the lights of evening change, the crowd drift past, and the moon.

The moon is gold.
The moon is cold.
The moon is old.
The man in the moon.
The moon is made of green cheese.
Oh, the moon is cool, so cool, the moon.

The man wonders if he will have a chance again next month; the man wonders if there are things he has forgotten, he wonders if there are things he never understood, he wonders ...

He wonders, now that he is alone and free ...

Now that he is free to wonder, he wonders:

What time it might possibly be, on the moon?

Blossoms

WHEN THEY TOOK HIM DOWNSTAIRS and laid him on the studio couch – which was a simple foldout bed – and turned his head so he could look out the bay window, one of them said that everything was in flower. Somebody else said, Yes, so far it has been the most beautiful summer she could remember. Yes, said another voice, a male voice this time, it has been, truly, a most beautiful summer. And then they left him, propped up on the pillows, his face turned towards the light that streamed through the window.

As he watched, the light slowly moved through the trees and the garden. Above the roof of the house across the way, the clouds, small, fluffy, white cumulus, ribbed with shifting blue shadows, moved with stately dignity through the one square of sky he could see; they moved as if they were delicately, inevitably, on their way somewhere else, somewhere terribly important, somewhere clouds go when they depart from the here and now.

The roof of the house across the way was dark burgundy slate. As the angle of the sun changed, the light on the slate came and went, like reflections of moonlight on the waves of a dark and tremulous sea. The shifting of the light and shadow, in the brightness of the summer day, was a form of music; it was a nocturne, being played just for him. Even at high noon, on that slate roof, there was a shifting, luminous, mysterious darkness. The darkness was a

depth into which he could plunge; he would doze, drift in and out of
sleep, and plunge deep into that warm imagined ocean, deep into
the shimmering mysteries, and come up, splashing, to the surface,
gasping for air. He was alive; he was a swimmer. The shifting light
was life.

On one part of the oceanic roof was a wooden deck with flowers hanging in clusters from the metal railing. He remembered
that he'd read somewhere that they had such deck-like structures
on top of the noble homes in Venice. On those wooden aeries –
he also remembered this for some reason – Venetian women of the
Renaissance used to go to bleach their waist-length hair blond by
exposing it – splayed out on tables or headrests he supposed – to
the sunlight, the watery Venetian sunlight that rained down out of
that watery blue Venetian sky so beautifully captured, as he remembered, by the Venetian painter Tiepolo.

Early each morning a woman came out onto the roof terrace. She
wore a long, flowered, freely floating dress that he supposed must be
some sort of nightgown or robe. It was strangely old-fashioned, the
way she was scantily but formally dressed. He pictured her body,
which he thought of as naked under the robe. He imagined the surfaces of her skin, exposed, feeling the drafty cool of the morning; he
imagined her feeling the morning air drifting under the loose robe;
he imagined her smooth skin, sloughing off the humid warmth of the
night, reborn and newly cool, voluptuously cool, as the woman offered
herself, like a priestess, to the virgin newness of the day.

Sometimes the woman lingered at the railing, her elbows on the
balustrade, her hands cupping a mug of coffee. She drank slowly,
as if savoring each sip, as if savoring each instant, as if savoring her
own body, each moment of her own life.

She was not young – she was perhaps fifty-five, maybe even sixty,
but to him she looked utterly young and desirable, and, between
sleep and waking, he imagined moving his hands up her thighs, and

he imagined how her skin would be cool and smooth, and then hot and damp, and how she would put her fingers in his hair, and clutch his hair and ...

And she would say things.

And she would call him by soft names, soft intimate names.

The mind wanders.

She was not aware that he existed, not aware that he was dying, not aware that he could see her, or that he thought about her, or that he imagined her ...

He remembered desire – vaguely, indistinctly, like the odor of an old perfume, lingering, almost fading away into nothingness, not quite.

He remembered that desire was the energy to imagine.

Imagination was the energy to desire.

Energy was the desire to ...

This was a thought, he realized, it was almost a thought.

It drifted away.

Thoughts ... He had lost the habit of having thoughts; the habit had been worn away by the years, by his routines, and his cowardice, and, now, by illness – by the final weakness that slows down every living thing, slower and slower, unto death.

Sometimes the woman in the roof garden, in her loose, flowing robe – he imagined the robe as something smooth, caressing, like silk or satin – watered the plants. Sometimes she stood by the railing, staring into space, for a long time, not even drinking, merely cupping the coffee mug in her hands.

Feelings, feelings and sensations – they now belonged to other bodies, to other people, and to memories, and to imagination, for his body was dying, almost dead – it could not be much longer now.

A man next door came and went. He was there to walk the neighbor's dog while the neighbor was away. The door opened with a click. And then the man would stand there for a moment, and he would whistle or call and the dog – invisible, too low to be seen from the bay window – would come limping along. He remembered how the dog walked – it was an old dog – and it moved with a lopsided, swaying delicate gait. The man talked to the dog and sometimes he heard snatches of conversation between the man and the dog. He imagined the man could see him, propped up on the studio couch, his face turned to the light. But he wasn't sure.

He did not want to die. He had done everything he could not to die. All the treatments had been followed, all the remedies exhausted, and all his money exhausted too. Now there was nothing.

Time passed. He must have slept.

He couldn't see them; but some people were just outside the window, two men, at least two men.

"The azaleas next to the bougainvillea, now, that's a bold stroke. Someone around here has real taste. See the way the yellow stands out against the ..."

He wondered who the person was. Then another voice ...

"There's an art to these things, you know, a definite art."

"Oh, yes."

"There is an art to living. It consists of little things."

"Yes. Life does consist of little things."

"That's life – little things."

"In the end, yes ..."

"Indeed, everything is, in the end, little things."

The voices faded. The men, whoever they were, went away.

Too bad he couldn't tell anybody about anything. But, no, it wasn't too bad. Talk was useless. Talk was vanity. People didn't listen. People didn't care. Besides, now, where he was going, or where he was about to go, there was nothing to say.

He was not afraid of death. Life, he had discovered, was the frightening thing; you can so easily fail at living. Living is like an exam. It is repeated, over and over. You can easily fail, over and over. He knew that he had failed and that he had missed his life. It was like missing a bus, he thought, and he would almost have smiled at the comparison, if he'd been able to smile. The last couple of months, when he'd tried to smile, what came was a rictus, and now it was like nothing at all. Once his smile had been considered charming, one of his best features. Yes, he'd missed the bus; he'd missed his life, his life had not been what he wanted it to be; he had wanted love, he had been hungry for it, thirsty for it, starving for it, but he was too proud to ask for it, too timid to earn it, too ignorant to know how to conquer it ...

Or maybe it was impossible anyway.

Maybe everyone around him had failed and lied about it just as he had.

Everyone was closed off from everyone else; everyone was imprisoned in pride, in solitude, in their death-in-life solitude. Most lives, he suspected, were mimicry of life, a pale copy.

He drifted off; he would sleep now; he would sleep.

∞

She sat down on the steps and as she lit the cigarette the wooden match flared with bitter, pungent burning. She inhaled and exhaled and closed her eyes.

Did she love him in the end? He was a cadaver, in the end, that's what he was, he was a burden, an obstacle; he was not something you could love. Dead people are not something you can love. Or can you? Now, she was bereft of everything, even of resentment. She was naked. It was as if she were naked, a wanton, naked little girl, or young woman. Her life, what she had thought of as her life, had been stripped away from her. It was his fault, really, yes, it was his fault – he had been incapable of love.

She had been young once, and she felt she should be young again – yes, by all rights she should be young again. She should be able to start everything all over, from scratch. She had not had a chance. She had offered herself to him so many times; but his spirit and body had been grudging, negligent, and stingy. She had fluttered around him, displaying all her treasures, all her charms, all her intelligence, but to no avail. He had robbed her of her life. Now, yes, she would like to start again. Why not? The spirit burns bright, even when the flesh ...

She had been a skinny little kid, full of angry energy.

She had a thin face – she thought, now seeing herself, as so often in the past, from the outside, seeing herself vividly, as if she were on a stage, or in a photograph – but it was a sensual face; it was austere, but wanton; it had hungry eyes, full lips – a beautiful smile, and an active and hungry mouth. Such contradictions, she had been told, could be very alluring. In the mirror, she had often looked at herself and wondered. What will become of you?

She had had a long rope of jet-black hair, too, hanging down her back to her waist, sometimes as far down as her waist. Yes, the most beautiful thing about her, they said, that's what they said, long ago – what beautiful hair!

Now it was a long rope of gray. She could still coil it around her neck, or shake it out like a horse's tail.

She sat hunched on the step, her knees up in front of her, her bare legs lightly tanned, smoking a cigarette. Life went up in smoke so easily. Smoke and fire, they were sacred symbols, natural metaphors. She breathed out; and a wreath of white smoke hung lazily in the air. It looked like a blossom, the way it curled, faded, insubstantial, and then was gone, an orchid perhaps, an exotic orchid. She looked up. Above her, blossoms twirled down from the trees through the bluish air.

This was the most beautiful summer in memory.

They all said so.

When someone was dead, they were just gone.

He had been dead long before he died.

She wondered what mistakes she had made. She had intended her life to be bright, violent, original and intense, above all, intense. She was going to do something with it – and what, in the end, had she done? She had done nothing. Oh, for a moment, it had seemed beautiful, for a moment it had been exciting, he starred on television, she produced, and she acted too, in two successful television series, and they had lunch in the best restaurants, they gossiped about all the right people, they were greeted everywhere with "darling" and "oh, darling, that was so brilliant last night ..." Then he got sick, his program was canceled; they went from party to party trying to get back into whatever it was they wanted back into ...

∞

"The flowers are almost all gone."

"Yes."

"They don't last long – do they?"

"No. "

The two men stood for a moment not saying anything. They really didn't know each other, so there was nothing much to say.

"The damned coffin was certainly difficult to get out the front door."

"Just think. If he'd been upstairs, it would have been impossible."

"That's why she had him brought down. It made it easier to die. "

"Easier to die," the man stroked his chin, "easier to be carried away."

"Yes."

They stood for a moment. The air was warm and moved against them, sensual and voluptuous, the lightest of summer breezes. A few fluffy bright white clouds moved slowly and happily through the high deep blue of the sky. Somewhere a lawn sprinkler began to move, hissing and swishing back and forth, just on the edge of hearing, almost subliminal.

Up on the roof terrace, opposite, a woman was standing, her elbows on the balustrade, cupping a coffee mug in her hands – it looked like a coffee mug. The light shifted, reflecting, on the slate roof of the large house – waves on a dark ocean. A cicada began to whir.

From one of the trees, a blossom detached itself.

It drifted slowly, gently down, for an instant brightly catching the light, until it reached the dark earth of a flowerbed. And there it lay.

"Even this beauty will end," said one of the men, glancing up at the sky.

"Yes." The other man glanced at the bright blossom. He had followed its progress: It had twirled down, making little arabesques, a work of art really, pirouetting like a flirtatious ballerina showing off, fluttering and swirling, as if resisting gravity, as if resisting the fall, as if resisting the end; and now it lay on the freshly turned, dark earth, the dark, sparking earth, which was so rich and so dark it consumed the light and seemed, like the blossom, to be waiting – tremulously waiting – with deep damp sensual anticipation, waiting for something immense, something meaningful, yes, waiting for something to happen ... "Yes, the blossom is waiting," thought the man, "but waiting for what?"

Now We Dance

GRANDMOTHER IS CRYING; mother looks sad and wipes her eyes; they have real feelings; we look at pictures.

Now the picture is all funny. It's in black and white though when I will remember it in future years I will think it was in color. But there was no color in those days. Static runs across the picture and squiggly lines and it hisses. The picture goes up and down with funny little lines and you can't really see it at all.

It's the antenna, mother says. It's the rain, it's the wind. There's a short, somebody says. Maybe the wires are loose, somebody else says. They take grandmother from the room. She is crying and she is bent and walks very slow.

I watch the picture. It says nothing. It makes a noise like a frying pan bubbling or a hissing snake. I go to the window. It is night. Rain makes thick smeared little lines sideways on the glass. I touch the glass. It is cold. I see my nose in the glass. I press my nose against the glass. I press my nose flat. It is cold. I can't see anything. There's nothing to see.

They won't open the coffin, somebody says.

No, says somebody.

The morticians did their best, says somebody. *Morticians*, I mouth the word silently and decide I will look it up: *morticians*. There is a book in mother's room with all the words in it.

My little sister sits on a chair in a pink dress. Her feet don't touch the floor. She has very small white shoes with gold buckles. I wonder how they can make shoes so small. She is watching the picture but there is nothing there but snow. She puts her hand in her mouth, all four fingers. When she was little and got mad she took her own shit out of her diapers and threw it all over her room on the walls where her crib was. Her room had high windows. It was summer. You could see the leaves. She looked happy in her crib. She bites her fist and swings her legs. She is tired of sitting in the chair and there is nothing in the picture but snow. Hissing snow.

Outside it is raining and it is cold.

He was in the water three days, says somebody.

The girl too, somebody says.

Carried downstream, somebody says.

If only it would stop raining. Somebody coughs.

∞

Somebody was crying. Then there were real pictures. I was looking at the pictures. A fat man was hitting a thin man. Both men wore hats. It was night. Not this night. Not now. Another night. "Horrible news," the man standing at the door said. My mother put her hand to the side of her face. She was wearing jeans and sandals and a T-shirt and had been reading a script and was holding it in her hand.

Pictures.

He's in the big box.

She's in the little box.

I see my face in the wood. Inside the box he is lying there but we can't see him. The mortician did the best he could, somebody says. *Mortician*, I repeat, *Mortician*. I touch the wood. It's cool. I let my fingers stay on the wood. Just the tips. Inside the box he is

lying there but we can't see him. I put my face close to the wood and
breathe and make a little cloud.

Mother has pictures in the basement in cardboard boxes. She
takes them out and looks at them. Except for you and your little
sister and granny, they were my only family, she says. Everybody is
dead, she says. I love you, she says, I love both of you, oh, so much.
The pictures are brown. A man is sitting on a donkey. Three men
are standing in a row. They have moustaches and are wearing vests.
One man is smoking a cigar. A woman is smiling. She is wearing a
beautiful dress. Mother puts the pictures back in the box.

They say she was going to marry him, someone says.

Him, with his daughter, and all.

She was beautiful, his daughter.

A tomboy, they say.

Her, with her own two girls, cute as buttons, and already widowed once.

The fates are unkind.

The gods shower their gifts, and then ...

They lived together already, out on her farm.

That film he wrote is coming out next month.

Yes, there's talk of a second Oscar.

A beautiful couple.

It was as if they were already married.

Widowed twice, then.

In the little box she is lying.

The box is closed. It is on some wooden sticks.

"How old was she?" somebody says.

"Eleven," says a voice, "small for her age."

"So young."

"The more's the pity."

I touch the wood. It is cool. She is inside. It is cool and smooth.

"Come down out of that tree," I say.
"Come and get me," she swings her legs.
She has brown legs and her dress is torn. I can see her panties
and a scab on her knee. I climb up the tree and we sit on the
branch and look at the house. "It's nice up here," she says. We
look at the house and the sun is warm.

I touch the wood of the box and the wood is cool and shiny and
she is inside. Candles are burning and make yellow light squiggles
on the shiny wood.

In the pictures on the screen there is a man in a boat, he is pol-
ing the boat through muddy water and I can see the roofs of houses,
the branches of trees, in the water, then there is a hiss and snow and
wiggly lines and nothing. My little sister is on the floor playing with
building blocks.

A flash flood, somebody says.
Yes, a freak storm.
One in a million chance.
Wrong place at the wrong time.
Yes.

They carry the two wooden boxes out. The men all wear black
suits. The sun hurts my eyes. I want to cry but I don't know why. His
box is the big one. Her box is the little one. Her box is small. My
little sister stays behind. "She's too young," says my mother, "She
doesn't understand." My mother takes my hand. "Come, Laura,"
she says.

"The water is warm," she says, "Come on in."
"No."
"Why?"

"I don't know. I don't feel like it."
"You never feel like anything, silly."
"That's not true."
"It is. I have to do everything first."
"You liar."
"I'm no liar."
She is thin and pale and in her underpants in the water; her shoulders and chest are all white and blue. The water is blue too. It's a picture.

They slide the boxes into the cars.

"I'll come in, I'll come in."
"Bet you won't!"
"Bet I will." I step into the cold water; it's not so cold. I shiver just the same.
"Come on, farther – scaredy-cat!"
I wade deeper and go under and when I come up I hear her laughter – tinkling like sunlight on waves.

The little box makes a hollow sound, sliding into the black car. The car is very long and has bright chrome. It is all polished. If you look close you can see the sky and trees and even yourself reflected in the polish, chrome and black. Mother takes my hand. My mother has very dark eyebrows. She is always very pale, her skin pure white. Her eyes are so dark when I look up into them. Her hand is dry. She smiles and squeezes my hand. My mother's hair is black and cut short almost like a boy's hair. She smiles and squeezes my hand. I squeeze her hand back. Her hand is smooth and strong. I like her hand and her fingers touching me, holding my hand.

The little box makes another hollow sound and now it's in the car. The man shuts the door of the car and we are in a car too. My mother touches her hair. "Granny's upset," she says, "she can't come." She puts her arm around my shoulder. The man driving the car is wearing a hat with a peak on it. The car starts and my mother is looking far away, her chin is high. It occurs to me that my mother is beautiful. People always look at her and say she is beautiful. Her photographs are in the newspapers and magazines. She's in movies. In the photographs she is always smiling. I think she is beautiful and I feel ashamed.

"I love your mom."
"My mom?"
"Huh, huh."
"You love her?"
"Huh, huh. She's beautiful."
"She's my mom."
"I know that, silly."
"And you're a girl."
"I know that, silly. It doesn't matter. Girls can love girls."

The car drives up the hill. My mother touches her eyes with a handkerchief. She puts on black glasses and I can't see her eyes. She smiles and her arm around my shoulders is tighter. The sun makes the leaves very bright.

The man with the cap gets out of the car and opens the door. My mother gets out and stands with her hand on the car roof and I look at her but I don't know if she sees me the glasses are so dark. The man with the cap is looking at her too. He looks worried. His forehead goes all wrinkled. He holds his cap in his hand. He opens his mouth. He is going to say something. My mother smiles and touches the edge of her glasses and puts her hand on my shoulder. She nods at the man with the cap and we leave him and start walking up through the leaves which are thick on the green grass and dry and bright and make a noise like breakfast cereal when our feet move through them. My mother has dark stockings and black shiny shoes with high heels. All the people, standing in rows, turn and look at mother; they bow their heads. Women touch their eyes with handkerchiefs. I see men with cameras and one woman but they are far away, among the gravestones.

The little box is at the edge of a hole in the ground.

And the big box is at the edge of another hole. Some colored leaves fall down swinging through the air and one lands on the big box and stays there. Black earth is piled beside the holes and smells like fields in spring.

I look at the little box. She is in the little box. A man with a funny collar says some words. He's the minister. He looks at my mother and bows. The little box is lowered down into the hole in the ground. I look down at it. My mother crouches next to me. She picks up a handful of earth and looks at me. I pick up some earth too. We throw the earth onto the box. The earth makes a hollow sound. Like a drum. I look at the box, all polished. It is a picture. She is in the box. She is a picture.

My mother stands up.

The big box is lowered into the ground. My mother kneels and throws earth on the box. I stand by her side. The big box is shiny with the dark splash of black earth on it. She stands up and touches me on the shoulder. "Laura," she says. We wait and my mother talks to people. From behind her black glasses, she smiles. She shakes hands. She kisses the women on the cheeks. I watch her and I think – they are not comforting her; she is comforting them.

We walk back to the car across the grass. The people are walking away. The man in the cap is waiting, standing beside the car. He holds his cap in his hands. I look back. The wind is in the trees, soft, like a song. I think: she is in a box in the earth; she is a picture. I look at pictures. Only days ago, it was. Time is so difficult to count. It was in the big attic room – with an old gramophone. She was going to teach me, she said. She was eleven.

> *"This is the way you dance," she says.*
> *"Like this?"*
> *"Here, hold my hand."*
> *"But I'm a girl."*
> *"It doesn't matter. We're both girls. And now we dance."*
> *"Like this?"*
> *"That's right. Stick your elbows out."*
> *"Like this?"*
> *"You're a genius, silly. Just right!"*
> *"Okay. I'm ready."*
> *"Now, stay there. I put on the record."*
> *"Now?"*
> *"Yes," she smiles, "Now. Now we dance."*

We are in the car. The trees go past. My hand is in my mother's hand. She squeezes my hand. "My little darling," she says. I close my eyes and I look at pictures: Yes, now I see, I look at pictures – *Yes, now we dance. Forever, we dance. Yes, forever we dance. It will never stop.*

Like an Angel

MOHAMMED HAD TO SMILE when the old woman said to him, "That's a very heavy backpack, young man."

"It is," he said, "It is." He hoped she didn't notice how much he was sweating and how the shoulder straps dug into his shoulders. He shifted the load uneasily.

The old woman sat down on a bench and opened a copy of *The Guardian* newspaper: "Home Secretary claims that ..."

The old woman's blouse was impeccably white, her skirt of some sort of tweed, and her shoes were of the sensible solid sort that old-fashioned Englishwomen seemed to wear for walking in the country. The paper made a slight crackling sound as she turned the pages.

Nothing else moved.

It was a hot, still day.

He could hear the crickets and the cicadas.

England was almost tropical now.

The air vibrated with golden light.

Mohammed turned away. The old women had a nice smile; he'd noticed how people's attitude to him had changed since he'd shaved off his beard and stopped wearing the skullcap and the gown. Now, they hardly gave him a second glance; now, often, people smiled and said "Good evening." Now, women looked at him in a new way, with interest, yes, with interest.

He was just a person now; dark-skinned, perhaps, but just a person.

A hot flush of shame rushed through him; it made him sweat even more; his clothes were sticking to him, all over, everywhere. The backpack *was* heavy, and wet and itchy; he wiggled his shoulders, trying to adjust the straps.

He looked up and down the platform.

The small country railway station dozed in the bright damp sunlight. The sky was a cloudless pale hazy blue; the bricks of the station shone a sleepy, dusty, red-and-yellow that made Mohammed blink and almost yawn; the green metal pedestrian bridge, 100 meters away, seemed suspended in the somnolent air, and, under it, the tracks curved away, shimmering and trembling, bluish-white in the morning heat. Somewhere, far away, a dog barked, a hollow, comforting sound, and Mohammed heard, briefly, a car accelerate and then the sound faded away.

Mohammed glanced at his watch.

Time moved slowly, as if in a dream.

Mohammed walked to the end of the platform and then back. Vines were growing over the brick wall, a bird called and another responded, and, from somewhere, a woman shouted for a child to come home. He twisted his shoulders and turned his neck, trying to make the backpack straps more comfortable. Sweat beaded his forehead. He wiped at it with the back of his hand.

The metal gate made a squeaking sound

Mohammed turned just in time to see a young woman hurrying onto the platform. She was carrying a thin black briefcase and was dressed in a stylish dark jacket, a dark short skirt, dark stockings, and black high-heeled shoes. She was blond and had pale skin and was wearing large dark sunglasses.

A lawyer, he thought, she must be a lawyer.

He'd seen lots of lawyers in his work, and lots of women lawyers,

bright, hard, stylish and ironic young English women who had little
time for the bearded, dark-skinned Muslim IT expert.

The young woman put down her briefcase, pulled out a cell
phone, punched a number, and waited. Catching his glance,
she smiled, shrugged, and turned away. "Hello, Michael, I
hate to do this to you, but I'm running late and ... No problem,
thanks, you're an angel. I owe you. I really do owe you. I'll see
you at about 11:30 or 12:00 ... Thanks ... Thanks again. Yes, I will ...
Thanks ... Cheers!"

She turned again, and smiled at Mohammed, apologetically –
perhaps for invading the quiet of the platform, sheepish perhaps at
having used the cell phone, or perhaps, she felt embarrassed – and
guilty – because she was late, and was sharing the fact of her sheepish guilt with him. She picked up her briefcase, walked to the edge
of the platform and stood there.

The immense high silence held the station platform in its grip.

The blue sky burned with brightness.

A cicada began to whirr: a vibrant rasping sound that made the
dry hot day seem even hotter, even drier.

Mohammed closed his eyes. There were so many voices in the
world; it was like music, so many voices, intermingling, intertwin-
ing, rising, and falling; people's lives were like the elements of a vast
symphony, with many melodies, like a rich fabric with all the threads
intertwined; if you took out one thread, then two, then three ... And
all the threads were intertwined in infinite ways. He thought: if you
cut through the cloth with scissors, the threads dangle, pointless,
unconnected ...

Death is like cutting through the cloth.

He had taken a bus to the small town and then had walked to the
railway station. In the bus he had watched the countryside pass by:
big green fields, rows of hedges, farm houses, woods, a few streams,
small villages, cattle and horses.

Imam Saladin had given them their missions. Mohammed was to take a bus out of the city and then across country to the little village of Helford. The Imam's finger had moved over the map. His fingernails, Mohammed noticed, were perfectly manicured, perfectly clean. In the village Mohammed was to board the train that went from West Egg to London. The Imam was so intense and so handsome that his dark face seemed to glow. He was a truly spiritual man.

"The train stops at a university town, a famous university town," the Imam had said, "and there will be some important people on the train, people who are on television often, giving their opinions on so many things."

"TV dons," said Mohammed.

"Yes, TV dons," said the Imam.

Mohammed nodded.

"When people are not faceless, it helps," said the Imam. "It is more effective. For the public it will be as if they lost a friend, a neighbor, someone they knew."

"Yes, certainly. I understand," said Mohammed.

"Suffering is not suffering when it is not understood," said the Imam, "Such is human nature. The suffering of strangers is not suffering. This must be personal, very personal."

"Yes," said Mohammed.

Mohammed had prepared by praying and fasting and praying and trying to purify himself. He had obeyed and, with reluctance, shaved off his beard and changed his residence. When he first looked in the mirror it occurred to him that without his beard he was handsome, in the way that a man on television or in films might be handsome. He was vaguely ashamed and embarrassed by this but it gave him pleasure too and he wondered at the pleasure it gave him and knew that such a form of self-consciousness, of self-adoration, was sinful and could easily lead him astray as he had seen so many other young men led astray, young men who drank and whored and gambled and drove expensive cars and frequented non-Muslim women, infidels.

It would all be very simple – all he had to do was push the button.

Then he would be a martyr.

Then he would be in paradise.

The new clothes felt strange, the tight jeans and T-shirt and the rimless glasses and the serious yet stylish shoes.

The train appeared around the bend. It was an ordinary suburban train, the sort that went through a dozen small towns, including the famous university town. It seemed to move slowly towards the station, the flat front of the train foreshortened in the shimmering heat, a hazy blue, as if it were a train in a dream; as if time were slowing down. The driver's face was a pale oval, a sketch of a face. Everything and everyone moved slowly; the world was an illusion, thought Mohammed, it was unreal, an illusion ...

The old woman got up, folded her *Guardian*, and stepped forward. The young woman lawyer moved closer to the edge of the platform. The flat front of the train moved nearer, became larger, and loomed up towards Mohammed.

The train came to a stop. Metal creaked, doors opened.

Mohammed climbed on board.

He sat down and put the backpack on the seat beside him.

The end of the cord with the button was just visible, hanging out of the flap.

The ticket collector was an older Sikh gentleman. He was heavyset, had a full salt and pepper beard and large, liquid, sad eyes that peered out, blinking, from behind his rimless glasses. He looked at Mohammed's ticket and he nodded, his eyes lingered for a moment on Mohammed and Mohammed held his gaze and nodded back.

The young woman lawyer sat down opposite Mohammed. She took off her dark sunglasses and glanced at him and smiled and looked down. Mohammed decided that she was an extraordinarily beautiful woman and he felt a twinge of lust and guilt and shame and he looked down. He looked up again. There was something about the purity of her face that reminded him of something. He tried to think what. *What* did she remind him of? She opened her briefcase and took out a few stapled papers and a ballpoint pen and began to make notes on one of the papers. The old lady, sitting across the aisle, opened up *The Guardian* and began, once again to read. She glanced over her glasses at Mohammed and smiled. He smiled back.

The train stopped at the famous university town and a number of people got on. One of them was a tall, thin, sharp-featured man Mohammed had seen on television. Yes, he was a TV don, a famous philosopher who seemed to be able to talk about any subject under the sun. Several other gentlemen who looked like professors or bankers got on and a young woman with two little girls, and then a group of teenage girls in plaid skirts and jackets – a school uniform, Mohammed decided. They made a lot of noise and were laughing and joking among themselves as they settled in at the far end of the car.

The car was becoming crowded. Mohammed stood up and took his backpack and offered his seat and the one next to it to the woman with the two little girls.

"Oh, thank you," she said, "that is very kind. These two are a handful, and if they aren't sitting down they will be running all over the car."

The old woman looked up from behind *The Guardian* and smiled at Mohammed, her eyes half-closing, as if to remind him how she admired him, carrying that heavy backpack, and giving the woman and her children his seat: an admirable young man, a true gentleman, standing up so that the woman and her two girls could sit down.

The Imam had said it was best to do it in the tunnel. "It will be much more effective that way," he said, "Rescue is difficult and the force of the explosion doubled. It will destroy virtually the whole train. There will be no escape."

As the train rounded a bend, and was about to enter the tunnel that had been chosen, the young woman lawyer, who had been absorbed in her documents, looked up, and focused, gazing, wide-eyed, straight at him. "You look pale. Are you alright?" There was concern in her eyes. "Here, you can take my seat."

Mohammed stared at her. Yes, she was beautiful, but what did she remind him of? What did she look like?

She started to get up. "I really think you should sit down," she said. Her blue eyes were very blue and the blond hair shone like spun gold. She looked like, she looked like ... Yes, it was true: She looked like an angel.

An angel.

The landscape – green fields, grazing cows, and a distant wood – disappeared and there was a new darkness as the train, moving fast now, plunged into the tunnel. The angel was standing next to Mohammed, smiling, her teeth and lips bright, her eyes brimming with compassion and interest, indicating the seat where he should take his place.

"You really should sit down," she said.

Mohammed smiled at her, and nodded, and said, "Thank you, I think I shall," and tightened his fingers and pushed the button.

I Hate Hats

THE NIGHT MY FATHER MARRIED MY MOTHER all his hair
fell out. I don't know what the explanation for this was, but the truth
of the matter is it never came back. This event greatly marked my
later life for I was a curly little fellow.

Indeed, my mother would bounce me up and down on her lap or
knee and tell everybody what a curly little fellow I was.

My secret fear was that at some point in my predestined life I
would cease to be curly.

But this apocalyptic day was far in the future as with considerable satisfaction I observed my father's discomfiture.

For I was in her lap, not he.

And I had the curls, he didn't.

I was being bounced ...

& Etc ...

But all feelings are ambivalent at the best of times and all situa-
tions are precarious, so even as I bounced up and down and felt her
fingers wander lovingly through my curliness, I suspected that some
day fate might have Pop's fate in store for me and that I would end
up bald as a billiard ball and banished irrevocably to outer darkness,
far from any female lap, let alone my mother's.

My father did not take kindly to his deprivation.

He felt it was a crying shame and an unpardonable crime to go uncovered in this sublunary world. So he always wore a hat. He wore a hat outside under the sun, he wore a hat inside when he was viciously cutting up his baked potatoes and slipping a slice of butter into their wounds, he wore a hat up to the moment he slipped under the covers and turned out the light. Then he would place the hat flat on the rug on the floor beside the bed so he could grab it first thing in the morning. If however he and mother intended to engage in marital congress he would keep his hat on just in case in her excitement – if she experienced any – she reached up and touched his hatless %$#@! Such a traumatic mishap would immediately bring any &$#@& and any *+}%% to a shuddering halt.

The need to wear a hat was one reason for sticking to the missionary position. In that position there is less likelihood that your hat will fall or fly or get pushed off. There are perhaps other positions in which your hat is even more secure but such positions we have been informed on good authority ex cathedra are unthinkable, indeed inconceivable, and not to be contemplated.

The hat in question was a gray fedora.

This dates this piece as a period piece.

A great day was the day my father decided that the time had come for me to wear a hat.

It was already night – and this was lucky because such deeds are best done in darkness.

It was a gray fedora.

We had just been to a large Seaside Fair and I was still dizzy from riding on the Roller Coaster and on the Ferris wheel and from eating candy floss.

It was just we two, out on a get-together-with-son and get-together-with-dad mission.

Out in the harbor visiting warships were lit up in festive outline with strings of white light bulbs.

I wondered about the sailors.

On the roller coaster and in the fun house my father held onto his hat. Nothing fazed him, though he was in a foul mood at the end of these exercises. Some experiences in life are perhaps best undergone without a hat. The fun house had obligingly provided synthetic cobwebs that tried to snatch his hat away, off from the top of his head. And gravity, on the roller coaster, got confused and at one point tried to send the hat to the moon which was invisible but undoubtedly lurking about. My father held on with both hands to the rim of the hat and saved the situation, though almost at the cost of going to the moon himself, with his hat.

Under the warlike ships the dark water sparkled in ribbons of white light like ripples of tinsel.

Flags in rows along the seafront snapped in the night breeze and the metal flagpoles rattled, tugged at by yearning, invisible wind-spirits.

The stars were invisible too because there were clouds covering the sky, wrapping the earth in a warm and soggy blanket.

The wind rose and carried smells of the salt and the sea and places far away and stimulated my curly Wanderlust.

My father held onto his hat.

I let my curls play in the breeze or the breeze play in my curls, for I was still a curly little fellow, though less little than once I was.

We were about to go home, to go home to mother. Now I didn't want to go home, and I didn't want to go home to mother. I glanced backwards, longingly, at the strings of lamp-bulbs silhouetting the ships in the harbor thinking – as I often did – that life was going on somewhere else, far, far, far away, far away from where I happened to be. Life chez nous wore a hat. It was battened down. It was under hatches. Briefly it occurred to me that I would perhaps carry this brilliant deadness everywhere and wherever I went, through life unto death forever and ever and Amen. It would be life in the bell jar. This was one of those unpleasant epiphanies that occur when the night is thick with caresses and the perfumes heavy with sensual promise. It was as if I were looking at things through a thick pane of polished and crystalline glass. The lights and colors were if anything even more brilliant through this glass than otherwise they would have been, just as the grass is greener, for cows, on the other side of the fence. Often I wanted to be a cow too; but that is another story and has very little to do with my attitude toward hats. Though, if one thinks about it, everything is connected, and all stories under the sun are really one single story, one long meandering interminable monologue, told by a stuttering, drooling, irascible philosophical idiot, crouched by the wood stove, on a winter night, with a spittoon handy within spitting reach.

Perhaps I shall be reincarnated as a ruminant. That is a consummation for which it would be worth changing one's religion; but maybe not – who knows what chewing a cud does to your soul, over the long haul. In any case, at that precise moment the wind was whipping my long Aquascutum raincoat around my shoulders and my knees. It was an annoying, exhilarating feeling, as if the winds were shouting, "Come on! Let's get the hell out of here! Come on! Let's get on the Road! Let's Sail Away ... Come on!!"

But Daddy was calling.

He was impatient to begin the trek home.

So, reluctantly, I turned from all those other worlds that were buzzing and glittering in my head, and, with my raincoat flapping around my shins and around my bent and shrunken shoulders, I traipsed slowly behind Daddy.

We got to the car, which was among many other cars in a huge parking lot, cars stretched off in every direction, their hoods and roofs reflecting the neon lights, blue, green, and red.

It was then that Daddy said he had a surprise for me.

He opened his door.

I opened my door.

We got into the car.

It was a portentous moment.

I felt I was about to be initiated into the mysteries.

It was a hat.

With considerable pleasure Daddy placed the hat on my head.

It came down and pushed out the points of my ears. Like wing flaps.

It covered up all my curls, every single one.

"There!" said Daddy, and leaned back and contemplated his work and knew it was good.

Now we both had hats.

He looked at me.

I looked at him.

For the first time since I had known him – and I had known him as long as I could remember – I saw a big fat grin on my Daddy's face.

"Now," said Daddy, "We can set off home." He turned the key, put the automobile into gear, and off we set into the warm windy night, heading toward Mummy. "Be sure to wear your hat to dinner," said Daddy.

Our automobile putted through the night, leaving all the other parked automobiles behind.

I rolled down the window.

For the first time in memory, without a visible curl to my name, I contemplated the night air laden with invisible allurements and forbidden magic, and rippling past the family vehicle.

When Daddy had got up enough speed to be totally occupied in controlling the ton of inert metal at his command, an idea drifted into my confused and humiliated cerebellum.

I lifted the hat off my head.

My ears popped back into shape – Ping! Ping!

My curls jumped up and began to wave in the breeze.

I held the hat out the window and let the breeze ripple its rim. It made a voracious vicious snapping sound: A hungry hat. Beyond my outstretched hand, beyond the rippling rim of the hat, the moonlit fields of early autumn floated off in unreal waves of perfumed silver to the dark woods, for by now we were in the country and by now the capricious moon had decided to appear.

The hat flapped.

Daddy turned his attention to the flapping.

"What are you doing, Son?" he asked.

But he was helpless: both hands were desperately gripping the wheel of our 1948 Dodge. As was his wont. He wasn't going to let that car get away from him.

"I'm testing the hat," said I.

"Don't," he said.

I think he saw the inevitable was in danger of occurring.

"She's prepared lentil soup," he said. "We can't be late."

Ha, ha, thought I – he's boxed himself in. With lentil soup waiting, we can't stop.

The dark woods beckoned.

Dark and deep.

I let go of the hat.

It flew off, spinning, into the night, flying, glad to be gone, toward the dark, perfumed fields.

My Daddy let out a Whoop! Of pure pain.

But he didn't stop. The old Dodge had smelled lentil soup and was going to get us home, come hell or high water.

Well, miraculously, we did successfully get home. "Hello, Honey Bun, we made it!"

He boxed my ears.

He shook me up and down like I was a milk shake, a fizz soda, or a cocktail. My brains were addled.

But to no avail.

My curls stood to attention while we slurped our lentil soup.

Mummy asked if my curls had enjoyed their outing at the Amusement Park.

My curls bounced up and down: Yes.

After lentils, Mummy bounced me up and down, on her lap. My curls bounced too. Daddy wore his hat and read the newspaper. But I noticed his hands were red and white and trembling, it was last week's newspaper, and he was holding it upside down. Little things betray a man.

It was no longer possible to buy me a hat. There is a tide in the affairs of men, which once it is lost ...

But Fortune's Wheel turns.

Years later I was totally curl-less.

Smooth as a light bulb and without a curl to my name I drifted desperately through the streets of life. How can one be loved without a curl to call one's own?

In truth I still had lots of curls.

But they were not in the right place.

Well, maybe not.

Anyway, they were not the sorts of curls one could bring up in public.

The sun burnt down on my cloudless dome.

The stars sparkled off my half-moon pate.

I bought a hat.

It was a white straw panama with a black ribbon around the crown and it was a moment of great humiliation I can tell you.

I was ashamed to go out.

I slunk down side streets in the shade, hoping no one would notice.

Sometimes I could not keep myself entirely hidden.

Then I noticed – people were noticing.

The people who noticed most were people of the female persuasion. Indeed, they stared at me, straight in the eye, as they had never stared before.

I stared back.

Often they continued to stare. Sometimes, embarrassed, they glanced away, then peeked back. Sometimes they shifted their eyes without moving a face-muscle: zip-zip, zip-zip, zip-zip, back and forth; almond eyes are particularly good at this sort of sport. Sometimes, when I caught them, they gave me a stony glazed look, opened their mouths slightly, and licked their lips. That half-open breathless mouth, those pink little tongues, those gleaming traces of saliva! What signs of panting passion! They just couldn't resist! They were curious: What is under that hat?

Perhaps Daddy was onto something. Is that possible? Is it conceivable that his designs upon me were benign?

I bought myself a porkpie hat, a Tyrolean hat, a straw boater, a Borsalino, a Napoleon hat, a dunce's cap, and a woolen pull-down with a pompom on top.

They continued to stare, but the quality of the stare changed according to which hat I was wearing.

I experimented. I hung about in public parks wearing a hat. I loitered on disreputable sidewalks clothed in a hat. I hung on wire-mesh fences, splayed like a bat, wearing my dunce's cap. I sat on the back of buses wearing my beret, an unlit Gauloise slouched hanging from the side of my downturned mouth. My Borsalino, spiced up with mirror glasses, a white jacket, a black silk shirt and a white tie, I toted into Little Italy. They treated me like one of the Family.

I can tell you, ladies and gentlemen, my success has been considerable.

Curiosity, you see, catches the pussycat, as the old tale has it. Yes, they all want to know what is under that hat. Also, women are invariably drawn to the ridiculous. So, if you don't want to be cruel – or if you do (women are also invariably drawn to cruelty, ugliness, and the hopelessly dissolute, take it from me) – put on a hat.

Acknowlegments

I'D LIKE TO THANK the many people who made these stories possible and over the years encouraged the author in his foolhardy enterprise: Anna Porter, Andra Sheffer, Chuck Shamata and Diane Shamata, Diana Leblanc, Bernice Landry, Mark Fenwick, Beverly Topping, Irene Tudisco, Jules Cashford, Wendy Trueman, Florence Treadwell, Elena Solari, Simona Barabesi, Afsun Qureshi, Martine Matus Siebert, Dianne Rinehart, Paola Pugliatti, Janie Yoon, Marie-Christine Dunham-Pratt, John Ralston Saul, Adrienne Clarkson, Ramsay Derry, Claudia Neri, Heather Reid, Professor Rinus Wortel, and Jennifer and Julia Hambleton, and many others too numerous to name.

Special thanks to Aaron Poochigian for permission to use his translation of the Sappho poem and to Tony Kline for permission to use the Rilke excerpt.

About the Author

GILBERT REID was born and raised in Canada, lived for thirty years in Europe, principally in England, France, and Italy, working as an economist in Paris, diplomat in London and Rome, and teacher of English and English literature at the University of Messina in Sicily. He was for eleven years director of the Canadian Cultural Center in Rome. He has written for *The Times Literary Supplement, The Globe and Mail, Flare,* and many other publications, as well as writing and presenting radio series – notably *Gilbert Reid's France* and *Gilbert Reid's Italy* – for CBC IDEAS, and he has written television series such as *For King and Empire* and *For King and Country,* and many others. He is the author of the short story collection *So This is Love: Lollipop and Other Stories,* originally published by Key Porter in Canada and by St. Martin's Press in the US, and coauthor, with Jacqueline Park, of the historical novel *Son of Two Fathers,* House of Anansi Press, 2019, which is set in the Italian Renaissance. Reid's series of science fiction novels, *Adventures of V,* featuring a charming, dark-eyed, shape-changing half-alien superheroine, will appear in the autumn of 2019.

CPSIA information can be obtained
at www.ICGtesting.com
Printed in the USA
LVHW091546241019
635167LV00003B/34/P

9 780995 310803